BEAUTY AND THE BEAST

AND OTHER CLASSIC STORIES

COLLINS
CLASSICS

William Collins
An imprint of HarperCollins*Publishers*
1 London Bridge Street
London SE1 9GF

WilliamCollinsBooks.com

This William Collins paperback edition published in
Great Britain in 2017

1

A catalogue record for this book
is available from the British Library

ISBN 978-0-00-823860-5

Classic Literature: Words and Phrases adapted from
Collins English Dictionary

Typesetting in Kalix by Palimpsest Book Production Limited,
Falkirk, Stirlingshire

Printed and bound in Great Britain by
Clays Ltd, St Ives plc

MIX
Paper from
responsible sources
FSC® C007454

FSC™ is a non-profit international organisation established to promote
the responsible management of the world's forests. Products carrying the
FSC label are independently certified to assure consumers that they come
from forests that are managed to meet the social, economic and
ecological needs of present and future generations,
and other controlled sources.

Find out more about HarperCollins and the environment at
www.harpercollins.co.uk/green

History of William Collins

In 1819, millworker William Collins from Glasgow, Scotland, set up a company for printing and publishing pamphlets, sermons, hymn books, and prayer books. That company was Collins and was to mark the birth of HarperCollins Publishers as we know it today. The long tradition of Collins dictionary publishing can be traced back to the first dictionary William co-published in 1825, *Greek and English Lexicon*. Indeed, from 1840 onwards, he began to produce illustrated dictionaries and even obtained a licence to print and publish the Bible.

Soon after, William published the first Collins novel; however, it was the time of the Long Depression, where harvests were poor, prices were high, potato crops had failed, and violence was erupting in Europe. As a result, many factories across the country were forced to close down and William chose to retire in 1846, partly due to the hardships he was facing.

Aged 30, William's son, William II, took over the business. A keen humanitarian with a warm heart and a generous spirit, William II was truly 'Victorian' in his outlook. He introduced new, up-to-date steam presses and published affordable editions of Shakespeare's works and *The Pilgrim's Progress*, making them available to the masses for the first time.

A new demand for educational books meant that success came with the publication of travel books, scientific books, encyclopedias, and dictionaries. This demand to be educated led to the later publication of atlases, and Collins also held the monopoly on scripture writing at the time.

In the 1860s Collins began to expand and diversify and the idea of 'books for the millions' was developed, although the phrase wasn't coined until 1907. Affordable editions of classical literature were published, and in 1903 Collins introduced 10 titles in their Collins Handy Illustrated Pocket Novels. These proved so popular that a few years later this had increased to an output of 50 volumes, selling nearly half a million in their year of publication. In the same year, The Everyman's Library was also instituted, with the idea of publishing an affordable library of the most important classical works, biographies, religious and philosophical treatments, plays, poems, travel, and adventure. This series eclipsed all competition at the time, and the introduction of paperback books in the 1950s helped to open that market and marked a high point in the industry.

HarperCollins is and has always been a champion of the classics, and the current Collins Classics series follows in this tradition – publishing classical literature that is affordable and available to all. Beautifully packaged, highly collectible, and intended to be reread and enjoyed at every opportunity.

CONTENTS

BEAUTY AND THE BEAST

AND OTHER CLASSIC STORIES

JEANNE-MARIE
LEPRINCE DE
BEAUMONT

BEAUTY AND THE BEAST

There was once a very rich merchant, who had six children, three sons, and three daughters; being a man of sense, he spared no cost for their education, but gave them all kinds of masters. His daughters were extremely handsome, especially the youngest; when she was little, everybody admired her, and called her *the little Beauty*; so that, as she grew up, she still went by the name of *Beauty*, which made her sisters very jealous. The youngest, as she was handsome, was also better than her sisters. The two eldest had a great deal of pride, because they were rich. They gave themselves ridiculous airs, and would not visit other merchants' daughters, nor keep company with any but persons of quality. They went out every day upon parties of pleasure, balls, plays, concerts, etc. and laughed at their youngest sister, because she spent the greatest part of her time in reading good books. As it was known that they were to have great fortunes, several eminent merchants made their addresses to them; but the two eldest said they would never marry, unless they could meet with a Duke, or an Earl at least. Beauty very civilly thanked them that courted her, and told them she was too young yet to marry, but chose to stay with her father a few years longer.

All at once the merchant lost his whole fortune, excepting a small country-house at a great distance from town, and told his children, with tears in his eyes, they must go there and work for their living. The two eldest answered that they would not leave the town, for they had several lovers, who they were sure would be glad to have them, though they had no fortune; but in this they were mistaken, for their lovers slighted and forsook them in their poverty. As they were not beloved on account of their pride, everybody said, "they do not deserve to be pitied, we are glad to see their pride humbled, let them go and give themselves quality airs in milking the cows and minding their dairy. But," added they, "we are extremely concerned for Beauty, she was such a charming, sweet-tempered creature, spoke so kindly to poor people, and was of such an affable, obliging disposition." Nay, several gentlemen would have married her, though they knew she had not a penny; but she told them she could not think of leaving her poor father in his misfortunes, but was determined to go along with him into the country to comfort and attend him. Poor Beauty at first was sadly grieved at the loss of her fortune; "but," she said to herself, "were I to cry ever so much, that would not make things better, I must try to make myself happy without a fortune." When they came to their country-house, the merchant and his three sons applied themselves to husbandry and tillage; and Beauty rose at four in the morning, and made haste to have the house clean, and breakfast ready for the family. In the beginning she found it very difficult, for she had not been used to work as a servant; but in less than two months she grew stronger and healthier than ever. After she had done her work, she read, played on the harpsichord, or else sung whilst she spun. On the contrary, her two sisters did not know how to spend their time; they got up at ten, and did nothing but saunter about the whole day, lamenting the loss of their fine clothes and acquaintance. "Do but see our youngest sister," said they one to the other, "what a poor, stupid, mean-spirited creature she is, to be contented with such an unhappy situation." The good merchant was of a quite different opinion; he knew very well that Beauty outshone her sisters, in her person as well as her mind, and admired her humility, industry, and patience; for her sisters not only left her all the work of the house to do, but insulted her every moment.

The family had lived about a year in this retirement when the merchant received a letter, with an account that a vessel, on board of which he had effects, was safely arrived. This news had liked to have turned the heads of the two eldest daughters, who immediately flattered themselves with the hopes of returning to town; for they were quite weary of a country life; and when they saw their father ready to set out, they begged of him to buy them new gowns, caps, rings, and all manner of trifles; but Beauty asked for nothing, for she thought to herself, that all the money her father was going to receive would scarce be sufficient to purchase everything her sisters wanted. "What will you have, Beauty?" said her father. "Since you are so kind as to think of me," answered she, "be so kind as to bring me a rose, for as none grow hereabouts, they are a kind of rarity." Not that Beauty cared for a rose, but she asked for something, lest she should seem by her example to condemn her sisters' conduct, who would have said she did it only to look particular. The good man went on his journey; but when he came there, they went to law with him about the merchandize, and after a great deal of trouble and pains to no purpose, he came back as poor as before.

He was within thirty miles of his own house, thinking on the pleasure he should have in seeing his children again, when going through a large forest he lost himself. It rained and snowed terribly, besides, the wind was so high, that it threw him twice off his horse; and night coming on, he began to apprehend being either starved to death with cold and hunger, or else devoured by the wolves, whom he heard howling all around him, when, on a sudden, looking through a long walk of trees, he saw a light at some distance, and going on a little farther, perceived it came from a palace illuminated from top to bottom. The merchant returned God thanks for this happy discovery, and hasted to the palace; but was greatly surprised at not meeting with anyone in the out-courts. His horse followed him, and seeing a large stable open, went in, and finding both hay and oats, the poor beast, who was almost famished, fell to eating very heartily. The merchant tied him up to the manger and walked towards the house, where he saw no one, but entering into a large hall, he found a good fire, and a table plentifully set out, with but one cover laid. As he was wet quite through with the rain and snow, he drew near the fire to dry himself. "I hope," said he, "the master of the house, or his servants, will excuse the liberty I take; I suppose it will not be long before some of them appear."

He waited a considerable time, till it struck eleven, and still nobody came: at last he was so hungry that he could stay no longer, but took a chicken and ate it in two mouthfuls, trembling all the while. After this, he drank a few glasses of wine, and growing more courageous, he went out of the hall, and crossed through several grand apartments with magnificent furniture, till he came into a chamber, which had an exceeding good bed in it, and as he was very much fatigued, and it was past midnight, he concluded it was best to shut the door, and go to bed.

It was ten the next morning before the merchant waked, and as he was going to rise, he was astonished to see a good suit of clothes in the room of his own, which were quite spoiled. "Certainly," said he, "this palace belongs to some kind fairy, who has seen and pitied my distress." He looked through a window, but instead of snow saw the most delightful arbours, interwoven with the most beautiful flowers that ever were beheld. He then returned to the great hall, where he had supped the night before, and found some chocolate ready made on a little table. "Thank you, good Madam Fairy," said he aloud, "for being so careful as to provide me a breakfast; I am extremely obliged to you for all your favours."

The good man drank his chocolate, and then went to look for his horse; but passing through an arbour of roses, he remembered Beauty's request to him, and gathered a branch on which were several; immediately he heard a great noise, and saw such a frightful beast coming towards him, that he was ready to faint away. "You are very ungrateful," said the beast to him, in a terrible voice, "I have saved your life by receiving you into my castle, and, in return, you steal my roses, which I value beyond anything in the universe; but you shall die for it; I give you but a quarter of an hour to prepare yourself, to say your prayers." The merchant fell on his knees, and lifted up both his hands: "My Lord," said he, "I beseech you to forgive me, indeed I had no intention to offend in gathering a rose for one of my daughters, who desired me to bring her one." "My name is not My Lord," replied the monster, "but Beast; I don't love compliments, not I; I like people should speak as they think; and so do not imagine I am to be moved by any of your flattering speeches; but you say you have got daughters; I will forgive you, on condition that one of them come willingly, and suffer for you. Let me have no words, but go about your business, and swear that if your daughter refuse to die in your stead, you will return within three months." The merchant had no mind to sacrifice his daughters to the ugly monster, but he thought, in obtaining this respite, he should have the satisfaction of seeing them once more; so he promised upon oath he would return, and the Beast told him he might set out when he pleased; "but," added he, "you shall not depart empty handed; go back to the room where you lay, and you will see a great empty chest; fill it with whatever you like best, and I will send it to your home," and at the same time Beast withdrew. "Well," said the good man to himself, "if I must die, I shall have the comfort, at least, of leaving something to my poor children."

He returned to the bed-chamber, and finding a great quantity of broad pieces of gold, he filled the great chest the Beast had mentioned, locked it, and afterwards took his horse out of the stable, leaving the palace with as much grief as he had entered it with joy. The horse, of his own accord, took one of the roads of the forest; and in a few hours the good man was at home. His children came around him, but, instead of receiving their embraces with pleasure, he looked on them, and, holding up the branch he had in his hands, he burst into tears. "Here, Beauty," said he, "take these roses; but little do you think how dear they are like to cost your unhappy father;" and then related his fatal adventure: immediately the two eldest set up lamentable outcries, and said all manner of ill-natured things to Beauty, who did not cry at all. "Do but see the pride of that little wretch," said they; "she would not ask for fine clothes, as we did; but no, truly, Miss wanted to distinguish herself; so now she will be the death of our poor father, and yet she does not so much as shed a tear." "Why should I," answered Beauty, "it would be very needless, for my father shall not suffer upon my account, since the monster will accept one of his daughters, I will deliver myself up to all his fury, and I am very happy in thinking that my death will save my father's life, and be a proof of my tender love for him." "No, sister," said her three brothers, "that shall not be, we will go find the monster, and either kill him, or perish in the attempt." "Do not imagine any such thing, my sons," said the merchant, "Beast's power is so great, that I have no hopes of your overcoming him; I am charmed with Beauty's kind and generous offer, but I cannot yield to it; I am old, and have not long to live, so can only lose a few years, which I regret for your sakes alone, my dear children." "Indeed, father," said Beauty, "you shall not go to the palace without me, you cannot hinder me from following you." It was to no purpose all they could say, Beauty still insisted on setting out for the fine palace; and her sisters were delighted at it, for her virtue and amiable qualities made them envious and jealous.

The merchant was so afflicted at the thoughts of losing his daughter, that he had quite forgot the chest full of gold; but at night, when he retired to rest, no sooner had he shut his chamber-door, than, to his great astonishment, he found it by his bedside; he was determined, however, not to tell his children that he was grown rich, because they would have wanted to return to town, and he was resolved not to leave the country; but he trusted Beauty with the secret, who informed him that two gentlemen came in his absence, and courted her sisters; she begged her father to consent to their marriage, and give them fortunes; for she was so good, that she loved them, and forgave them heartily all their ill-usage. These wicked creatures rubbed their eyes with an onion, to force some tears when they parted with their sister; but her brothers were really concerned. Beauty was the only one who did not shed tears at parting, because she would not increase their uneasiness.

The horse took the direct road to the palace; and towards evening they perceived it illuminated as at first: the horse went of himself into the stable, and the good man and his daughter came into the great hall, where they found a table splendidly served up, and two covers. The merchant had no heart to eat; but Beauty endeavoured to appear cheerful, sat down to table, and helped him. Afterwards, thought she to herself, "Beast surely has a mind to fatten me before he eats me, since he provides such a plentiful entertainment." When they had supped, they heard a great noise, and the merchant, all in tears, bid his poor child farewell, for he thought Beast was coming. Beauty was sadly terrified at his horrid form, but she took courage as well as she could, and the monster having asked her if she came willingly; "y—e—s," said she, trembling. "You are very good, and I am greatly obliged to you; honest man, go your ways tomorrow morning, but never think of returning here again. Farewell, Beauty." "Farewell, Beast," answered she; and immediately the monster withdrew. "Oh, daughter," said the merchant, embracing Beauty, "I am almost frightened to death; believe me, you had better go back, and let me stay here." "No, father," said Beauty, in a resolute tone, "you shall set out tomorrow morning, and leave me to the care and protection of Providence." They went to bed, and thought they should not close their eyes all night; but scarce were they laid down, than they fell fast asleep; and Beauty dreamed a fine lady came, and said to her, "I am content, Beauty, with your good will; this good action of yours, in giving up your own life to save your father's, shall not go unrewarded." Beauty waked, and told her father her dream, and though it helped to comfort him a little, yet he could not help crying bitterly when he took leave of his dear child.

As soon as he was gone, Beauty sat down in the great hall, and fell a crying likewise; but as she was mistress of a great deal of resolution, she recommended herself to God, and resolved not to be uneasy the little time she had to live; for she firmly believed Beast would eat her up that night.

However, she thought she might as well walk about till then, and view this fine castle, which she could not help admiring; it was a delightful pleasant place, and she was extremely surprised at seeing a door, over which was wrote, "BEAUTY'S APARTMENT." She opened it hastily, and was quite dazzled with the magnificence that reigned throughout; but what chiefly took up her attention was a large library, a harpsichord, and several music books. "Well," said she to herself, "I see they will not let my time hang heavy on my hands for want of amusement." Then she reflected, "Were I but to stay here a day, there would not have been all these preparations." This consideration inspired her with fresh courage; and opening the library, she took a book, and read these words in letters of gold:—

"Welcome, Beauty, banish fear,
You are queen and mistress here;
Speak your wishes, speak your will,
Swift obedience meets them still."

"Alas," said she, with a sigh, "there is nothing I desire so much as to see my poor father, and to know what he is doing." She had no sooner said this, when casting her eyes on a great looking-glass, to her great amazement she saw her own home, where her father arrived with a very dejected countenance; her sisters went to meet him, and, notwithstanding their endeavours to appear sorrowful, their joy, felt for having got rid of their sister, was visible in every feature: a moment after, everything disappeared, and Beauty's apprehensions at this proof of Beast's complaisance.

At noon she found dinner ready, and while at table, was entertained with an excellent concert of music, though without seeing anybody: but at night, as she was going to sit down to supper, she heard the noise Beast made; and could not help being sadly terrified. "Beauty," said the monster, "will you give me leave to see you sup?" "That is as you please," answered Beauty, trembling. "No," replied the Beast, "you alone are mistress here; you need only bid me be gone, if my presence is troublesome, and I will immediately withdraw: but tell me, do not you think me very ugly?" "That is true," said Beauty, "for I cannot tell a lie; but I believe you are very good-natured." "So I am," said the monster, "but then, besides my ugliness, I have no sense; I know very well that I am a poor, silly, stupid creature." "'Tis no sign of folly to think so," replied Beauty, "for never did fool know this, or had so humble a conceit of his own understanding." "Eat then, Beauty," said the monster, "and endeavour to amuse yourself in your palace; for everything here is yours, and I should be very uneasy if you were not happy." "You are very obliging," answered Beauty; "I own I am pleased with your kindness, and when I consider that, your deformity scarce appears." "Yes, yes," said the Beast, "my heart is good, but still I am a monster." "Among mankind," says Beauty, "there are many that deserve that name more than you, and I prefer you, just as you are, to those, who, under a human form, hide a treacherous, corrupt, and ungrateful heart." "If I had sense enough," replied the Beast,

"I would make a fine compliment to thank you, but I am so dull, that I can only say, I am greatly obliged to you." Beauty ate a hearty supper, and had almost conquered her dread of the monster; but she had liked to have fainted away, when he said to her, "Beauty, will you be my wife?" She was some time before she durst answer; for she was afraid of making him angry, if she refused. At last, however, she said, trembling, "No, Beast." Immediately the poor monster began to sigh, and hissed so frightfully, that the whole palace echoed. But Beauty soon recovered her fright, for Beast having said, in a mournful voice, "then farewell, Beauty," left the room; and only turned back, now and then, to look at her as he went out.

When Beauty was alone, she felt a great deal of compassion for poor Beast. "Alas," said she, "'tis a thousand pities anything so good-natured should be so ugly."

Beauty spent three months very contentedly in the palace: every evening Beast paid her a visit, and talked to her during supper, very rationally, with plain good common sense, but never with what the world calls wit; and Beauty daily discovered some valuable qualifications in the monster; and seeing him often, had so accustomed her to his deformity, that, far from dreading the time of his visit, she would often look on her watch to see when it would be nine; for the Beast never missed coming at that hour. There was but one thing that gave Beauty any concern, which was that every night, before she went to bed, the monster always asked her if she would be his wife. One day she said to him, "Beast, you make me very uneasy, I wish I could consent to marry you, but I am too sincere to make you believe that will ever happen: I shall always esteem you as a friend; endeavour to be satisfied with this." "I must," said the Beast, "for, alas! I know too well my own misfortune; but then I love you with the tenderest affection: however, I ought to think myself happy that you will stay here; promise me never to leave me." Beauty blushed at these words; she had seen in her glass, that her father had pined himself sick for the loss of her, and she longed to see him again. "I could," answered she, "indeed promise never to leave you entirely, but I have so great a desire to see my father, that I shall fret to death, if you refuse me that satisfaction." "I had rather die myself," said the monster, "than give you the least uneasiness: I will send you to your father, you shall remain with him, and poor Beast will die with grief." "No," said Beauty, weeping, "I love you too well to be the cause of your death: I give you my promise to return in a week: you have shewn me that my sisters are married, and my brothers gone to the army; only let me stay a week with my father, as he is alone." "You shall be there tomorrow morning," said the Beast, "but remember your promise: you need only lay your ring on the table before you go to bed, when you have a mind to come back: farewell, Beauty." Beast sighed as usual, bidding her good night; and Beauty went to bed very sad at seeing him so afflicted. When she waked the next morning, she found herself at her father's, and having rang a little bell that was by her bed-side, she saw the maid come; who, the moment she saw her, gave a loud shriek; at which the good man ran upstairs, and thought he should have died with joy to see his dear daughter again. He held her fast locked in his arms above a quarter of an hour. As soon as the first transports were over, Beauty began to think of rising, and was afraid she had no clothes to put on; but the maid told her, that she had just found, in the next room, a large trunk full of gowns, covered with gold and diamonds. Beauty thanked good Beast for his kind care, and taking one of the plainest of them, she intended to make a present of the others to her sisters. She scarce had said so, when the trunk disappeared. Her father told her, that Beast insisted on her keeping them herself; and immediately both gowns and trunk came back again.

Beauty dressed herself; and in the meantime they sent to her sisters, who hasted thither with their husbands. They were both of them very unhappy. The eldest had married a gentleman, extremely handsome indeed, but so fond of his own person, that he was full of nothing but his own dear self, and neglected his wife. The second had married a man of wit, but he only made use of it to plague and torment everybody, and his wife most of all. Beauty's sisters sickened with envy, when they saw her dressed like a Princess, and more beautiful than ever; nor could all her obliging affectionate behaviour stifle their jealousy, which was ready to burst when she told them how happy she was. They went down into the garden to vent it in tears; and said one to the other, "In what is this little creature better than us, that she should be so much happier?" "Sister," said the eldest, "a thought just strikes my mind; let us endeavour to detain her above a week, and perhaps the silly monster will be so enraged at her for breaking her word, that he will devour her." "Right, sister," answered the other, "therefore we must shew her as much kindness as possible." After they had taken this resolution, they went up, and behaved so affectionately to their sister, that poor Beauty wept for joy. When the week was expired, they cried and tore their hair, and seemed so sorry to part with her, that she promised to stay a week longer.

In the meantime, Beauty could not help reflecting on herself for the uneasiness she was likely to cause poor Beast, whom she sincerely loved, and really longed to see again. The tenth night she spent at her father's, she dreamed she was in the palace garden, and that she saw Beast extended on the grass-plot, who seemed just expiring, and, in a dying voice, reproached her with her ingratitude. Beauty started out of her sleep and bursting into tears, "Am not I very wicked," said she, "to act so unkindly to Beast, that has studied so much to please me in everything? Is it his fault that he is so ugly, and has so little sense? He is kind and good, and that is sufficient. Why did I refuse to marry him? I should be happier with the monster than my sisters are with their husbands; it is neither wit nor a fine person in a husband, that makes a woman happy; but virtue, sweetness of temper, and complaisance: and Beast has all these valuable qualifications. It is true, I do not feel the tenderness of affection for him, but I find I have the highest gratitude, esteem, and friendship; and I will not make him miserable; were I to be so ungrateful, I should never forgive myself." Beauty having said this, rose, put her ring on the table, and then laid down again; scarce was she in bed before she fell asleep; and when she waked the next morning, she was over-joyed to find herself in the Beast's palace. She put on one of her richest suits to please him, and waited for evening with the utmost impatience; at last the wished-for hour came, the clock struck nine, yet no Beast appeared. Beauty then feared she had been the cause of his death; she ran crying and wringing her hands all about the palace, like one in despair; after having sought for him every where, she recollected her dream, and flew to the canal in the garden, where she dreamed she saw him. There she found poor Beast stretched out, quite senseless, and, as she imagined, dead. She threw herself upon him without any dread, and finding his heart beat still, she fetched some water from the canal, and poured it on his head. Beast opened his eyes, and said to Beauty, "You forgot your promise, and I was so afflicted for having lost you, that I resolved to starve myself; but since I have the happiness of seeing you once more, I die satisfied." "No, dear Beast," said Beauty, "you must not die; live to be my husband; from this moment I give you my hand, and swear to be none but yours. Alas! I thought I had only a friendship for you, but the grief I now feel convinces me that I cannot live without you." Beauty scarcely had pronounced these words, when she saw the palace sparkle with light; and fireworks, instruments of music, everything seemed to give notice of some great event: but nothing could fix her attention; she turned to her dear Beast, for whom she trembled with fear; but how great was her surprise! Beast had disap-peared, and she saw, at her feet, one of the loveliest Princes that eye ever beheld, who returned her thanks for having put an end to the charm, under which he had so long resembled a Beast. Though this Prince was worthy of all her attention, she could not forbear asking where Beast was. "You see him at your feet," said the Prince: "a wicked fairy had condemned me to remain under that shape till a beautiful virgin should consent to marry me: the fairy likewise enjoined me to conceal my understanding; there was only you in the world generous enough to be won by the goodness of my temper; and in offering you my crown, I can't discharge the obligations I have to you." Beauty, agreeably surprised, gave the charming Prince her hand to rise; they went together into the castle, and Beauty was overjoyed to find, in the great hall, her father and his whole family, whom the beautiful lady, that appeared to her in her dream, had conveyed thither.

"Beauty," said this lady, "come and receive the reward of your judicious choice; you have preferred virtue before either wit or beauty, and deserve to find a person in whom all these qualifications are united: you are going to be a great Queen; I hope the throne will not lessen your virtue, or make you forget yourself. As to you, ladies," said the Fairy to Beauty's two sisters, "I know your hearts, and all the malice they contain: become two statues; but, under this transformation, still retain your reason. You shall stand before your sister's palace gate, and be it your punishment to behold her happiness; and it will not be in your power to return to your former state till you own your faults; but I am very much afraid that you will always remain statues. Pride, anger, gluttony, and idleness, are sometimes conquered, but the conversion of a malicious and envious mind is a kind of miracle." Immediately the fairy gave a stroke with her wand, and in a moment all that were in the hall were transported into the Prince's palace. His subjects received him with joy; he married Beauty, and lived with her many years; and their happiness, as it was founded on virtue, was complete.

HANS CHRISTIAN ANDERSEN

THE UGLY DUCKLING

It was lovely summer weather in the country, and the golden corn, the green oats, and the haystacks piled up in the meadows looked beautiful. The stork walking about on his long red legs chattered in the Egyptian language, which he had learnt from his mother. The corn-fields and meadows were surrounded by large forests, in the midst of which were deep pools. It was, indeed, delightful to walk about in the country. In a sunny spot stood a pleasant old farm-house close by a deep river, and from the house down to the water side grew great burdock leaves, so high, that under the tallest of them a little child could stand upright. The spot was as wild as the centre of a thick wood. In this snug retreat sat a duck on her nest, watching for her young brood to hatch; she was beginning to get tired of her task, for the little ones were a long time coming out of their shells, and she seldom had any visitors. The other ducks liked much better to swim about in the river than to climb the slippery banks, and sit under a burdock leaf, to have a gossip with her. At length one shell cracked, and then another, and from each egg came a living creature that lifted its head and cried, "Peep, peep." "Quack, quack," said the mother, and then they all quacked as well as they could, and looked about them on every side at the large green leaves. Their mother allowed them to look as much as they liked, because green is good for the eyes. "How large the world is," said the young ducks, when they found how much more room they now had than while they were inside the egg-shell. "Do you imagine this is the whole world?" asked the mother; "Wait till you have seen the garden; it stretches far beyond that to the parson's field, but I have never ventured to such a distance. Are you all out?" she continued, rising; "No, I declare, the largest egg lies there still. I wonder how long this is to last, I am quite tired of it;" and she seated herself again on the nest.

"Well, how are you getting on?" asked an old duck, who paid her a visit.

"One egg is not hatched yet," said the duck, "it will not break. But just look at all the others, are they not the prettiest little ducklings you ever saw? They are the image of their father, who is so unkind, he never comes to see."

"Let me see the egg that will not break," said the duck; "I have no doubt it is a turkey's egg. I was persuaded to hatch some once, and after all my care and trouble with the young ones, they were afraid of the water. I quacked and clucked, but all to no purpose. I could not get them to venture in. Let me look at the egg. Yes, that is a turkey's egg; take my advice, leave it where it is and teach the other children to swim."

"I think I will sit on it a little while longer," said the duck; "as I have sat so long already, a few days will be nothing."

"Please yourself," said the old duck, and she went away.

At last the large egg broke, and a young one crept forth crying, "Peep, peep." It was very large and ugly. The duck stared at it and exclaimed, "It is very large and not at all like the others. I wonder if it really is a turkey. We shall soon find it out, however when we go to the water. It must go in, if I have to push it myself."

On the next day the weather was delightful, and the sun shone brightly on the green burdock leaves, so the mother duck took her young brood down to the water, and jumped in with a splash. "Quack, quack," cried she, and one after another the little ducklings jumped in. The water closed over their heads, but they came up again in an instant, and swam about quite prettily with their legs paddling under them as easily as possible, and the ugly duckling was also in the water swimming with them.

"Oh," said the mother, "that is not a turkey; how well he uses his legs, and how upright he holds himself! He is my own child, and he is not so very ugly after all if you look at him properly. Quack, quack! come with me now, I will take you into grand society, and introduce you to the farmyard, but you must keep close to me or you may be trodden upon; and, above all, beware of the cat."

When they reached the farmyard, there was a great disturbance, two families were fighting for an eel's head, which, after all, was carried off by the cat. "See, children, that is the way of the world," said the mother duck, whetting her beak, for she would have liked the eel's head herself. "Come, now, use your legs, and let me see how well you can behave. You must bow your heads prettily to that old duck yonder; she is the highest born of them all, and has Spanish blood, therefore, she is well off. Don't you see she has a red flag tied to her leg, which is something very grand, and a great honour for a duck; it shows that every one is anxious not to lose her, as she can be recognized both by man and beast. Come, now, don't turn your toes, a well-bred duckling spreads his feet wide apart, just like his father and mother, in this way; now bend your neck, and say 'quack.'"

The ducklings did as they were bid, but the other duck stared, and said, "Look, here comes another brood, as if there were not enough of us already! and what a queer looking object one of them is; we don't want him here," and then one flew out and bit him in the neck.

"Let him alone," said the mother; "he is not doing any harm."

"Yes, but he is so big and ugly," said the spiteful duck "and therefore he must be turned out."

"The others are very pretty children," said the old duck, with the rag on her leg, "all but that one; I wish his mother could improve him a little."

"That is impossible, your grace," replied the mother; "he is not pretty; but he has a very good disposition, and swims as well or even better than the others. I think he will grow up pretty, and perhaps be smaller; he has remained too long in the egg, and therefore his figure is not properly formed;" and then she stroked his neck and smoothed the feathers, saying, "It is a drake, and therefore not of so much consequence. I think he will grow up strong, and able to take care of himself."

"The other ducklings are graceful enough," said the old duck. "Now make yourself at home, and if you can find an eel's head, you can bring it to me."

And so they made themselves comfortable; but the poor duckling, who had crept out of his shell last of all, and looked so ugly, was bitten and pushed and made fun of, not only by the ducks, but by all the poultry. "He is too big," they all said, and the turkey cock, who had been born into the world with spurs, and fancied himself really an emperor, puffed himself out like a vessel in full sail, and flew at the duckling, and became quite red in the head with passion, so that the poor little thing did not know where to go, and was quite miserable because he was so ugly and laughed at by the whole farmyard. So it went on from day to day till it got worse and worse. The poor duckling was driven about by every one; even his brothers and sisters were unkind to him, and would say, "Ah, you ugly creature, I wish the cat would get you," and his mother said she wished he had never been born. The ducks pecked him, the chickens beat him, and the girl who fed the poultry kicked him with her feet. So at last he ran away, frightening the little birds in the hedge as he flew over the palings.

"They are afraid of me because I am ugly," he said. So he closed his eyes, and flew still further, until he came out on a large moor, inhabited by wild ducks. Here he remained the whole night, feeling very tired and sorrowful.

In the morning, when the wild ducks rose in the air, they stared at their new comrade. "What sort of a duck are you?" they all said, coming round him.

He bowed to them, and was as polite as he could be, but he did not reply to their question. "You are exceedingly ugly," said the wild ducks, "but that will not matter if you do not want to marry one of our family."

Poor thing! he had no thoughts of marriage; all he wanted was permission to lie among the rushes, and drink some of the water on the moor. After he had been on the moor two days, there came two wild geese, or rather goslings, for they had not been out of the egg long, and were very saucy. "Listen, friend," said one of them to the duckling, "you are so ugly, that we like you very well. Will you go with us, and become a bird of passage? Not far from here is another moor, in which there are some pretty wild geese, all unmarried. It is a chance for you to get a wife; you may be lucky, ugly as you are."

"Pop, pop," sounded in the air, and the two wild geese fell dead among the rushes, and the water was tinged with blood. "Pop, pop," echoed far and wide in the distance, and whole flocks of wild geese rose up from the rushes. The sound continued from every direction, for the sportsmen surrounded the moor, and some were even seated on branches of trees, overlooking the rushes. The blue smoke from the guns rose like clouds over the dark trees, and as it floated away across the water, a number of sporting dogs bounded in among the rushes, which bent beneath them wherever they went. How they terrified the poor duckling! He turned away his head to hide it under his wing, and at the same moment a large terrible dog passed quite near him. His jaws were open, his tongue hung from his mouth, and his eyes glared fearfully. He thrust his nose close to the duckling, showing his sharp teeth, and then, "splash, splash," he went into the water without touching him, "Oh," sighed the duckling, "how thankful I am for being so ugly; even a dog will not bite me." And so he lay quite still, while the shot rattled through the rushes, and gun after gun was fired over him. It was late in the day before all became quiet, but even then the poor young thing did not dare to move. He waited quietly for several hours, and then, after looking carefully around him, hastened away from the moor as fast as he could. He ran over field and meadow till a storm arose, and he could hardly struggle against it. Towards evening, he reached a poor little cottage that seemed ready to fall, and only remained standing because it could not decide on which side to fall first. The storm continued so violent, that the duckling could go no further; he sat down by the cottage, and then he noticed that the door was not quite closed in consequence of one of the hinges having given way. There was therefore a narrow opening near the bottom large enough for him to slip through, which he did very quietly, and got a shelter for the night. A woman, a tom cat, and a hen lived in this cottage. The tom cat, whom the mistress called, "My little son," was a great favourite; he could raise his back, and purr, and could even throw out sparks from his fur if it were stroked the wrong way. The hen had very short legs, so she was called "Chickie short legs." She laid good eggs, and her mistress loved her as if she had been her own child. In the morning, the strange visitor was discovered, and the tom cat began to purr, and the hen to cluck.

"What is that noise about?" said the old woman, looking round the room, but her sight was not very good; therefore, when she saw the duckling she thought it must be a fat duck, that had strayed from home. "Oh what a prize!" she exclaimed, "I hope it is not a drake, for then I shall have some duck's eggs. I must wait and see." So the duckling was allowed to remain on trial for three weeks, but there were no eggs. Now the tom cat was the master of the house, and the hen was mistress, and they always said, "We and the world," for they believed themselves to be half the world, and the better half too. The duckling thought that others might hold a different opinion on the subject, but the hen would not listen to such doubts. "Can you lay eggs?" she asked. "No." "Then have the goodness to hold your tongue." "Can you raise your back, or purr, or throw out sparks?" said the tom cat. "No." "Then you have no right to express an opinion when sensible people are speaking." So the duckling sat in a corner, feeling very low spirited, till the sunshine and the fresh air came into the room through the open door, and then he began to feel such a great longing for a swim on the water, that he could not help telling the hen.

"What an absurd idea," said the hen. "You have nothing else to do, therefore you have foolish fancies. If you could purr or lay eggs, they would pass away."

"But it is so delightful to swim about on the water," said the duckling, "and so refreshing to feel it close over your head, while you dive down to the bottom."

"Delightful, indeed!" said the hen, "why you must be crazy! Ask the cat, he is the cleverest animal I know, ask him how he would like to swim about on the water, or to dive under it, for I will not speak of my own opinion; ask our mistress, the old woman – there is no one in the world more clever than she is. Do you think she would like to swim, or to let the water close over her head?"

"You don't understand me," said the duckling.

"We don't understand you? Who can understand you, I wonder? Do you consider yourself more clever than the cat, or the old woman? I will say nothing of myself. Don't imagine such nonsense, child, and thank your good fortune that you have been received here. Are you not in a warm room, and in society from which you may learn something. But you are a chatterer, and your company is not very agreeable. Believe me, I speak only for your own good. I may tell you unpleasant truths, but that is a proof of my friendship. I advise you, therefore, to lay eggs, and learn to purr as quickly as possible."

"I believe I must go out into the world again," said the duckling.

"Yes, do," said the hen. So the duckling left the cottage, and soon found water on which it could swim and dive, but was avoided by all other animals, because of its ugly appearance. Autumn came, and the leaves in the forest turned to orange and gold. Then, as winter approached, the wind caught them as they fell and whirled them in the cold air. The clouds, heavy with hail and snow-flakes, hung low in the sky, and the raven stood on the ferns crying, "Croak, croak." It made one shiver with cold to look at him. All this was very sad for the poor little duckling. One evening, just as the sun set amid radiant clouds, there came a large flock of beautiful birds out of the bushes. The duckling had never seen any like them before. They were swans, and they curved their graceful necks, while their soft plumage shown with dazzling whiteness. They uttered a singular cry, as they spread their glorious wings and flew away from those cold regions to warmer countries across the sea. As they mounted higher and higher in the air, the ugly little duckling felt quite a strange sensation as he watched them. He whirled himself in the water like a wheel, stretched out his neck towards them, and uttered a cry so strange that it frightened himself. Could he ever forget those beautiful, happy birds; and when at last they were out of his sight, he dived under the water, and rose again almost beside himself with excitement. He knew not the names of these birds, nor where they had flown, but he felt towards them as he had never felt for any other bird in the world. He was not envious of these beautiful creatures, but wished to be as lovely as they. Poor ugly creature, how gladly he would have lived even with the ducks had they only given him encouragement. The winter grew colder and colder; he was obliged to swim about on the water to keep it from freezing, but every night the space on which he swam became smaller and smaller. At length it froze so hard that the ice in the water crackled as he moved, and the duckling had to paddle with his legs as well as he could, to keep the space from closing up. He became exhausted at last, and lay still and helpless, frozen fast in the ice.

Early in the morning, a peasant, who was passing by, saw what had happened. He broke the ice in pieces with his wooden shoe, and carried the duckling home to his wife. The warmth revived the poor little creature; but when the children wanted to play with him, the duckling thought they would do him some harm; so he started up in terror, fluttered into the milk-pan, and splashed the milk about the room. Then the woman clapped her hands, which frightened him still more. He flew first into the butter-cask, then into the meal-tub, and out again. What a condition he was in! The woman screamed, and struck at him with the tongs; the children laughed and screamed, and tumbled over each other, in their efforts to catch him; but luckily he escaped. The door stood open; the poor creature could just manage to slip out among the bushes, and lie down quite exhausted in the newly fallen snow.

It would be very sad, were I to relate all the misery and privations which the poor little duckling endured during the hard winter; but when it had passed, he found himself lying one morning in a moor, amongst the rushes. He felt the warm sun shining, and heard the lark singing, and saw that all around was beautiful spring. Then the young bird felt that his wings were strong, as he flapped them against his sides, and rose high into the air. They bore him onwards, until he found himself in a large garden, before he well knew how it had happened. The apple-trees were in full blossom, and the fragrant elders bent their long green branches down to the stream which wound round a smooth lawn. Everything looked beautiful, in the freshness of early spring. From a thicket close by came three beautiful white swans, rustling their feathers, and swimming lightly over the smooth water. The duckling remembered the lovely birds, and felt more strangely unhappy than ever.

"I will fly to those royal birds," he exclaimed, "and they will kill me, because I am so ugly, and dare to approach them; but it does not matter: better be killed by them than pecked by the ducks, beaten by the hens, pushed about by the maiden who feeds the poultry, or starved with hunger in the winter."

Then he flew to the water, and swam towards the beautiful swans. The moment they espied the stranger, they rushed to meet him with outstretched wings.

"Kill me," said the poor bird; and he bent his head down to the surface of the water, and awaited death.

But what did he see in the clear stream below? His own image; no longer a dark, grey bird, ugly and disagreeable to look at, but a graceful and beautiful swan. To be born in a duck's nest, in a farmyard, is of no consequence to a bird, if it is hatched from a swan's egg. He now felt glad at having suffered sorrow and trouble, because it enabled him to enjoy so much better all the pleasure and happiness around him; for the great swans swam round the new-comer, and stroked his neck with their beaks, as a welcome.

Into the garden presently came some little children, and threw bread and cake into the water.

"See," cried the youngest, "there is a new one;" and the rest were delighted, and ran to their father and mother, dancing and clapping their hands, and shouting joyously, "There is another swan come; a new one has arrived."

Then they threw more bread and cake into the water, and said, "The new one is the most beautiful of all; he is so young and pretty." And the old swans bowed their heads before him.

Then he felt quite ashamed, and hid his head under his

wing; for he did not know what to do, he was so happy, and yet not at all proud. He had been persecuted and despised for his ugliness, and now he heard them say he was the most beautiful of all the birds. Even the elder-tree bent down its bows into the water before him, and the sun shone warm and bright. Then he rustled his feathers, curved his slender neck, and cried joyfully, from the depths of his heart, "I never dreamed of such happiness as this, while I was an ugly duckling."

THE EMPEROR'S NEW SUIT

Many, many years ago lived an emperor, who thought so much of new clothes that he spent all his money in order to obtain them; his only ambition was to be always well dressed. He did not care for his soldiers, and the theatre did not amuse him; the only thing, in fact, he thought anything of was to drive out and show a new suit of clothes. He had a coat for every hour of the day; and as one would say of a king "He is in his cabinet," so one could say of him, "The emperor is in his dressing-room."

The great city where he resided was very gay; every day many strangers from all parts of the globe arrived. One day two swindlers came to this city; they made people believe that they were weavers, and declared they could manufacture the finest cloth to be imagined. Their colours and patterns, they said, were not only exceptionally beautiful, but the clothes made of their material possessed the wonderful quality of being invisible to any man who was unfit for his office or unpardonably stupid.

"That must be wonderful cloth," thought the emperor. "If I were to be dressed in a suit made of this cloth I should be able to find out which men in my empire were unfit for their places, and I could distinguish the clever from the stupid.

I must have this cloth woven for me without delay." And he gave a large sum of money to the swindlers, in advance, that they should set to work without any loss of time. They set up two looms, and pretended to be very hard at work, but they did nothing whatever on the looms. They asked for the finest silk and the most precious gold-cloth; all they got they did away with, and worked at the empty looms till late at night.

"I should very much like to know how they are getting on with the cloth," thought the emperor. But he felt rather uneasy when he remembered that he who was not fit for his office could not see it. Personally, he was of opinion that he had nothing to fear, yet he thought it advisable to send some-body else first to see how matters stood. Everybody in the town knew what a remarkable quality the stuff possessed, and all were anxious to see how bad or stupid their neighbours were.

"I shall send my honest old minister to the weavers," thought the emperor. "He can judge best how the stuff looks, for he is intelligent, and nobody understands his office better than he."

The good old minister went into the room where the swindlers sat before the empty looms. "Heaven preserve us!" he thought, and opened his eyes wide, "I cannot see anything at all," but he did not say so. Both swindlers requested him to come near, and asked him if he did not admire the exqui-site pattern and the beautiful colours, pointing to the empty looms. The poor old minister tried his very best, but he could see nothing, for there was nothing to be seen. "Oh dear," he thought, "can I be so stupid? I should never have thought so, and nobody must know it! Is it possible that I am not fit for my office? No, no, I cannot say that I was unable to see the cloth."

"Now, have you got nothing to say?" said one of the swindlers, while he pretended to be busily weaving.

"Oh, it is very pretty, exceedingly beautiful," replied the

old minister looking through his glasses. "What a beautiful pattern, what brilliant colours! I shall tell the emperor that I like the cloth very much."

"We are pleased to hear that," said the two weavers, and described to him the colours and explained the curious pattern. The old minister listened attentively, that he might relate to the emperor what they said; and so he did.

Now the swindlers asked for more money, silk and gold-cloth, which they required for weaving. They kept everything for themselves, and not a thread came near the loom, but they continued, as hitherto, to work at the empty looms.

Soon afterwards the emperor sent another honest courtier to the weavers to see how they were getting on, and if the cloth was nearly finished. Like the old minister, he looked and looked but could see nothing, as there was nothing to be seen.

"Is it not a beautiful piece of cloth?" asked the two swindlers, showing and explaining the magnificent pattern, which, however, did not exist.

"I am not stupid," said the man. "It is therefore my good appointment for which I am not fit. It is very strange, but I must not let any one know it;" and he praised the cloth, which he did not see, and expressed his joy at the beautiful colours and the fine pattern. "It is very excellent," he said to the emperor.

Everybody in the whole town talked about the precious cloth. At last the emperor wished to see it himself, while it was still on the loom. With a number of courtiers, including the two who had already been there, he went to the two clever swindlers, who now worked as hard as they could, but without using any thread.

"Is it not magnificent?" said the two old statesmen who had been there before. "Your Majesty must admire the colours and the pattern." And then they pointed to the empty looms, for they imagined the others could see the cloth.

"What is this?" thought the emperor, "I do not see anything at all. That is terrible! Am I stupid? Am I unfit to be emperor? That would indeed be the most dreadful thing that could happen to me."

"Really," he said, turning to the weavers, "your cloth has our most gracious approval;" and nodding contentedly he looked at the empty loom, for he did not like to say that he saw nothing. All his attendants, who were with him, looked and looked, and although they could not see anything more than the others, they said, like the emperor, "It is very beautiful." And all advised him to wear the new magnificent clothes at a great procession which was soon to take place. "It is magnificent, beautiful, excellent," one heard them say; everybody seemed to be delighted, and the emperor appointed the two swindlers "Imperial Court weavers."

The whole night previous to the day on which the procession was to take place, the swindlers pretended to work, and burned more than sixteen candles. People should see that they were busy to finish the emperor's new suit. They pretended to take the cloth from the loom, and worked about in the air with big scissors, and sewed with needles without thread, and said at last: "The emperor's new suit is ready now."

The emperor and all his barons then came to the hall; the swindlers held their arms up as if they held something in their hands and said: "These are the trousers!" "This is the coat!" and "Here is the cloak!" and so on. "They are all as light as a cobweb, and one must feel as if one had nothing at all upon the body; but that is just the beauty of them."

"Indeed!" said all the courtiers; but they could not see anything, for there was nothing to be seen.

"Does it please your Majesty now to graciously undress," said the swindlers, "that we may assist your Majesty in putting on the new suit before the large looking-glass?"

The emperor undressed, and the swindlers pretended to

put the new suit upon him, one piece after another; and the emperor looked at himself in the glass from every side.

"How well they look! How well they fit!" said all. "What a beautiful pattern! What fine colours! That is a magnificent suit of clothes!"

The master of the ceremonies announced that the bearers of the canopy, which was to be carried in the procession, were ready.

"I am ready," said the emperor. "Does not my suit fit me marvellously?" Then he turned once more to the looking-glass, that people should think he admired his garments.

The chamberlains, who were to carry the train, stretched their hands to the ground as if they lifted up a train, and pretended to hold something in their hands; they did not like people to know that they could not see anything.

The emperor marched in the procession under the beautiful canopy, and all who saw him in the street and out of the windows exclaimed: "Indeed, the emperor's new suit is incomparable! What a long train he has! How well it fits him!" Nobody wished to let others know he saw nothing, for then he would have been unfit for his office or too stupid. Never emperor's clothes were more admired.

"But he has nothing on at all," said a little child at last. "Good heavens! listen to the voice of an innocent child," said the father, and one whispered to the other what the child had said. "But he has nothing on at all," cried at last the whole people. That made a deep impression upon the emperor, for it seemed to him that they were right; but he thought to himself, "Now I must bear up to the end." And the chamberlains walked with still greater dignity, as if they carried the train which did not exist.

THE LITTLE MERMAID

Far out in the ocean, where the water is as blue as the prettiest cornflower, and as clear as crystal, it is very, very deep;
so deep, indeed, that no cable could fathom it: many church
steeples, piled one upon another, would not reach from the
ground beneath to the surface of the water above. There dwell
the Sea King and his subjects. We must not imagine that there
is nothing at the bottom of the sea but bare yellow sand. No,
indeed; the most singular flowers and plants grow there; the
leaves and stems of which are so pliant, that the slightest
agitation of the water causes them to stir as if they had life.
Fishes, both large and small, glide between the branches, as
birds fly among the trees here upon land. In the deepest spot
of all, stands the castle of the Sea King. Its walls are built of
coral, and the long, gothic windows are of the clearest amber.
The roof is formed of shells, that open and close as the water
flows over them. Their appearance is very beautiful, for in
each lies a glittering pearl, which would be fit for the diadem
of a queen.

The Sea King had been a widower for many years, and
his aged mother kept house for him. She was a very wise
woman, and exceedingly proud of her high birth; on that
account she wore twelve oysters on her tail; while others, also

of high rank, were only allowed to wear six. She was, however, deserving of very great praise, especially for her care of the little sea-princesses, her grand-daughters. They were six beautiful children; but the youngest was the prettiest of them all; her skin was as clear and delicate as a rose-leaf, and her eyes as blue as the deepest sea; but, like all the others, she had no feet, and her body ended in a fish's tail. All day long they played in the great halls of the castle, or among the living flowers that grew out of the walls. The large amber windows were open, and the fish swam in, just as the swallows fly into our houses when we open the windows, excepting that the fishes swam up to the princesses, ate out of their hands, and allowed themselves to be stroked. Outside the castle there was a beautiful garden, in which grew bright red and dark blue flowers, and blossoms like flames of fire; the fruit glittered like gold, and the leaves and stems waved to and fro continually. The earth itself was the finest sand, but blue as the flame of burning sulphur. Over everything lay a peculiar blue radiance, as if it were surrounded by the air from above, through which the blue sky shone, instead of the dark depths of the sea. In calm weather the sun could be seen, looking like a purple flower, with the light streaming from the calyx. Each of the young princesses had a little plot of ground in the garden, where she might dig and plant as she pleased. One arranged her flower-bed into the form of a whale; another thought it better to make hers like the figure of a little mermaid; but that of the youngest was round like the sun, and contained flowers as red as his rays at sunset. She was a strange child, quiet and thoughtful; and while her sisters would be delighted with the wonderful things which they obtained from the wrecks of vessels, she cared for nothing but her pretty red flowers, like the sun, excepting a beautiful marble statue. It was the representation of a handsome boy, carved out of pure white stone, which had fallen to the bottom of the sea from a wreck. She planted by the statue a rose-coloured weeping willow. It grew splendidly, and very soon hung its fresh branches over the statue, almost down to the blue sands. The shadow had a violet tint, and waved to and fro like the branches; it seemed as if the crown of the tree and the root were at play, and trying to kiss each other. Nothing gave her so much pleasure as to hear about the world above the sea. She made her old grandmother tell her all she knew of the ships and of the towns, the people and the animals. To her it seemed most wonderful and beautiful to hear that the flowers of the land should have fragrance, and not those below the sea; that the trees of the forest should be green; and that the fishes among the trees could sing so sweetly, that it was quite a pleasure to hear them. Her grandmother called the little birds fishes, or she would not have understood her; for she had never seen birds.

"When you have reached your fifteenth year," said the grand-mother, "you will have permission to rise up out of the sea, to sit on the rocks in the moonlight, while the great ships are sailing by; and then you will see both forests and towns."

In the following year, one of the sisters would be fifteen: but as each was a year younger than the other, the youngest would have to wait five years before her turn came to rise up from the bottom of the ocean, and see the earth as we do. However, each promised to tell the others what she saw on her first visit, and what she thought the most beautiful; for their grandmother could not tell them enough; there were so many things on which they wanted information. None of them longed so much for her turn to come as the youngest, she who had the longest time to wait, and who was so quiet and thoughtful. Many nights she stood by the open window, looking up through the dark blue water, and watching the fish as they splashed about with their fins and tails. She could see the moon and stars shining faintly; but through the water they looked larger than they do to our eyes. When something like a black cloud passed between her and them, she knew that it was either a whale swimming over her head, or a ship full of human beings, who never imagined that a pretty little mermaid was standing beneath them, holding out her white hands towards the keel of their ship.

As soon as the eldest was fifteen, she was allowed to rise to the surface of the ocean. When she came back, she had hundreds of things to talk about; but the most beautiful, she said, was to lie in the moonlight, on a sandbank, in the quiet sea, near the coast, and to gaze on a large town nearby, where the lights were twinkling like hundreds of stars; to listen to the sounds of the music, the noise of carriages, and the voices of human beings, and then to hear the merry bells peal out from the church steeples; and because she could not go near to all those wonderful things, she longed for them more than ever. Oh, did not the youngest sister listen eagerly to all these descriptions? and afterwards, when she stood at the open window looking up through the dark blue water, she thought of the great city, with all its bustle and noise, and even fancied she could hear the sound of the church bells, down in the depths of the sea.

In another year the second sister received permission to rise to the surface of the water, and to swim about where she pleased. She rose just as the sun was setting, and this, she said, was the most beautiful sight of all. The whole sky looked like gold, while violet and rose-coloured clouds, which she could not describe, floated over her; and, still more rapidly than the clouds, flew a large flock of wild swans towards the setting sun, looking like a long white veil across the sea. She also swam towards the sun; but it sunk into the waves, and the rosy tints faded from the clouds and from the sea.

The third sister's turn followed; she was the boldest of them all, and she swam up a broad river that emptied itself into the sea. On the banks she saw green hills covered with beautiful vines; palaces and castles peeped out from amid the proud trees of the forest; she heard the birds singing, and the rays of the sun were so powerful that she was obliged often to dive down under the water to cool her burning face. In a narrow creek she found a whole troop of little human children, quite naked, and sporting about in the water; she wanted to play with them, but they fled in a great fright; and then a little black animal came to the water; it was a dog, but she did not know that, for she had never before seen one. This animal barked at her so terribly that she became frightened, and rushed back to the open sea. But she said she should never forget the beautiful forest, the green hills, and the pretty little children who could swim in the water, although they had not fish's tails.

The fourth sister was more timid; she remained in the midst of the sea, but she said it was quite as beautiful there as nearer the land. She could see for so many miles around her, and the sky above looked like a bell of glass. She had seen the ships, but at such a great distance that they looked like sea-gulls. The dolphins sported in the waves, and the great whales spouted water from their nostrils till it seemed as if a hundred fountains were playing in every direction.

The fifth sister's birthday occurred in the winter; so when her turn came, she saw what the others had not seen the first time they went up. The sea looked quite green, and large icebergs were floating about, each like a pearl, she said, but larger and loftier than the churches built by men. They were of the most singular shapes, and glittered like diamonds. She had seated herself upon one of the largest, and let the wind play with her long hair, and she remarked that all the ships sailed by rapidly, and steered as far away as they could from the iceberg, as if they were afraid of it. Towards evening, as the sun went down, dark clouds covered the sky, the thunder rolled and the lightning flashed, and the red light glowed on the icebergs as they rocked and tossed on the heaving sea. On all the ships the sails were reefed with fear and trembling, while she sat calmly on the floating iceberg, watching the blue lightning, as it darted its forked flashes into the sea.

When first the sisters had permission to rise to the surface, they were each delighted with the new and beautiful sights they saw; but now, as grown-up girls, they could go when they pleased, and they had become indifferent about it. They wished themselves back again in the water, and after a month had passed they said it was much more beautiful down below, and pleasanter to be at home. Yet often, in the evening hours, the five sisters would twine their arms round each other, and rise to the surface, in a row. They had more beautiful voices than any human being could have; and before the approach of a storm, and when they expected a ship would be lost, they swam before the vessel, and sang sweetly of the delights to be found in the depths of the sea, and begging the sailors not to fear if they sank to the bottom. But the sailors could not understand the song, they took it for the howling of the storm. And these things were never to be beautiful for them; for if the ship sank, the men were drowned, and their dead bodies alone reached the palace of the Sea King.

When the sisters rose, arm-in-arm, through the water in this way, their youngest sister would stand quite alone, looking after them, ready to cry, only that the mermaids have no tears, and therefore they suffer more. "Oh, were I but fifteen years old," said she: "I know that I shall love the world up there, and all the people who live in it."

At last she reached her fifteenth year. "Well, now, you are grown up," said the old dowager, her grandmother; "so you must let me adorn you like your other sisters;" and she placed a wreath of white lilies in her hair, and every flower leaf was half a pearl. Then the old lady ordered eight great oysters to attach themselves to the tail of the princess to show her high rank.

"But they hurt me so," said the little mermaid.

"Pride must suffer pain," replied the old lady. Oh, how

gladly she would have shaken off all this grandeur, and laid aside the heavy wreath! The red flowers in her own garden would have suited her much better, but she could not help herself: so she said, "Farewell," and rose as lightly as a bubble to the surface of the water. The sun had just set as she raised her head above the waves; but the clouds were tinted with crimson and gold, and through the glimmering twilight beamed the evening star in all its beauty. The sea was calm, and the air mild and fresh. A large ship, with three masts, lay becalmed on the water, with only one sail set; for not a breeze stiffed, and the sailors sat idle on deck or amongst the rigging. There was music and song on board; and, as darkness came on, a hundred coloured lanterns were lighted, as if the flags of all nations waved in the air. The little mermaid swam close to the cabin windows; and now and then, as the waves lifted her up, she could look in through clear glass window-panes, and see a number of well-dressed people within. Among them was a young prince, the most beautiful of all, with large black eyes; he was sixteen years of age, and his birthday was being kept with much rejoicing. The sailors were dancing on deck, but when the prince came out of the cabin, more than a hundred rockets rose in the air, making it as bright as day. The little mermaid was so startled that she dived under water; and when she again stretched out her head, it appeared as if all the stars of heaven were falling around her, she had never seen such fireworks before. Great suns spurted fire about, splendid fireflies flew into the blue air, and everything was reflected in the clear, calm sea beneath. The ship itself was so brightly illuminated that all the people, and even the smallest rope, could be distinctly and plainly seen. And how handsome the young prince looked, as he pressed the hands of all present and smiled at them, while the music resounded through the clear night air.

It was very late; yet the little mermaid could not take her eyes from the ship, or from the beautiful prince. The coloured lanterns had been extinguished, no more rockets rose in the air, and the cannon had ceased firing; but the sea became restless, and a moaning, grumbling sound could be heard beneath the waves: still the little mermaid remained by the cabin window, rocking up and down on the water, which enabled her to look in. After a while, the sails were quickly unfurled, and the noble ship continued her passage; but soon the waves rose higher, heavy clouds darkened the sky, and lightning appeared in the distance. A dreadful storm was approaching; once more the sails were reefed, and the great ship pursued her flying course over the raging sea. The waves rose mountains high, as if they would have overtopped the mast; but the ship dived like a swan between them, and then rose again on their lofty, foaming crests. To the little mermaid this appeared pleasant sport; not so to the sailors. At length the ship groaned and creaked; the thick planks gave way under the lashing of the sea as it broke over the deck; the mainmast snapped asunder like a reed; the ship lay over on her side; and the water rushed in. The little mermaid now perceived that the crew were in danger; even she herself was obliged to be careful to avoid the beams and planks of the wreck which lay scattered on the water. At one moment it was so pitch dark that she could not see a single object, but a flash of lightning revealed the whole scene; she could see every one who had been on board excepting the prince; when the ship parted, she had seen him sink into the deep waves, and she was glad, for she thought he would now be with her; and then she remembered that human beings could not live in the water, so that when he got down to her father's palace he would be quite dead. But he must not die. So she swam about among the beams and planks which strewed the surface of the sea, forgetting that they could crush her to pieces. Then she dived deeply under the dark waters, rising and falling with the waves, till at length she managed to reach the young prince, who was fast losing the power of swimming in that stormy sea. His limbs were failing him, his beautiful eyes were closed, and he would have died had not the little mermaid come to his assistance. She held his head above the water, and let the waves drift them where they would.

In the morning the storm had ceased; but of the ship not a single fragment could be seen. The sun rose up red and glowing from the water, and its beams brought back the hue of health to the prince's cheeks; but his eyes remained closed. The mermaid kissed his high, smooth forehead, and stroked back his wet hair; he seemed to her like the marble statue in her little garden, and she kissed him again, and wished that he might live. Presently they came in sight of land; she saw lofty blue mountains, on which the white snow rested as if a flock of swans were lying upon them. Near the coast were beautiful green forests, and close by stood a large building, whether a church or a convent she could not tell. Orange and citron trees grew in the garden, and before the door stood lofty palms. The sea here formed a little bay, in which the water was quite still, but very deep; so she swam with the handsome prince to the beach, which was covered with fine, white sand, and there she laid him in the warm sunshine, taking care to raise his head higher than his body. Then bells sounded in the large white building, and a number of young girls came into the garden. The little mermaid swam out further from the shore and placed herself between some high rocks that rose out of the water; then she covered her head and neck with the foam of the sea so that her little face might not be seen, and watched to see what would become of the poor prince. She did not wait long before she saw a young girl approach the spot where he lay. She seemed frightened at first, but only for a moment; then she fetched a number of people, and the mermaid saw that the prince came to life again, and smiled upon those who stood round him. But to her he sent no smile; he knew not that she had saved him. This made her very unhappy, and when he was led away into the great building, she dived down sorrowfully into the water, and returned to her father's castle. She had always been silent and thoughtful, and now she was more so than ever. Her sisters asked her what she had seen during her first visit to the surface of the water; but she would tell them nothing. Many an evening and morning did she rise to the place where she had left the prince. She saw the fruits in the garden ripen till they were gathered, the snow on the tops of the mountains melt away; but she never saw the prince, and therefore she returned home, always more sorrowful than before. It was her only comfort to sit in her own little garden, and fling her arm round the beautiful marble statue which was like the prince; but she gave up tending her flowers, and they grew in wild confusion over the paths, twining their long leaves and stems round the branches of the trees, so that the whole place became dark and gloomy. At length she could bear it no longer, and told one of her sisters all about it. Then the others heard the secret, and very soon it became known to two mermaids whose intimate friend happened to know who the prince was. She had also seen the festival on board ship, and she told them where the prince came from, and where his palace stood.

"Come, little sister," said the other princesses; then they entwined their arms and rose up in a long row to the surface of the water, close by the spot where they knew the prince's palace stood. It was built of bright yellow shining stone, with long flights of marble steps, one of which reached quite down to the sea. Splendid gilded cupolas rose over the roof, and between the pillars that surrounded the whole building stood life-like statues of marble. Through the clear crystal of the lofty windows could be seen noble rooms, with costly silk curtains and hangings of tapestry; while the walls were covered with beautiful paintings which were a pleasure to look at. In the centre of the largest saloon a fountain threw its sparkling jets high up into the glass cupola of the ceiling, through which the sun shone down upon the water and upon the beautiful plants growing round the basin of the fountain. Now that she knew where he lived, she spent many an evening and many a night on the water near the palace. She would swim much nearer the shore than any of the others ventured to do; indeed once she went quite up the narrow channel under the marble balcony, which threw a broad shadow on the water. Here she would sit and watch the young prince, who thought himself quite alone in the bright moonlight. She saw him many times of an evening sailing in a pleasant boat, with music playing and flags waving. She peeped out from among the green rushes, and if the wind caught her long silvery-white veil, those who saw it believed it to be a swan, spreading out its wings. On many a night, too, when the fishermen, with their torches, were out at sea, she heard them relate so many good things about the doings of the young prince, that she was glad she had saved his life when he had been tossed about half-dead on the waves. And she remembered that his head had rested on her bosom, and how heartily she had kissed him; but he knew nothing of all this, and could not even dream of her. She grew more and more fond of human beings, and wished more and more to be able to wander about with those whose world seemed to be so much larger than her own. They could fly over the sea in ships, and mount the high hills which were far above the clouds; and the lands they possessed, their woods and their fields, stretched far away beyond the reach of her sight. There was so much that she wished to know, and her sisters were unable to answer all her questions. Then she applied to her old grandmother, who knew all about the upper world, which she very rightly called the lands above the sea.

"If human beings are not drowned," asked the little mermaid, "can they live forever? do they never die as we do here in the sea?"

"Yes," replied the old lady, "they must also die, and their term of life is even shorter than ours. We sometimes live to three hundred years, but when we cease to exist here we only become the foam on the surface of the water, and we have not even a grave down here of those we love. We have not immortal souls, we shall never live again; but, like the green sea-weed, when once it has been cut off, we can never flourish more. Human beings, on the contrary, have a soul which lives forever, lives after the body has been turned to dust. It rises up through the clear, pure air beyond the glittering stars. As we rise out of the water, and behold all the land of the earth, so do they rise to unknown and glorious regions which we shall never see."

"Why have not we an immortal soul?" asked the little mermaid mournfully; "I would give gladly all the hundreds of years that I have to live, to be a human being only for one day, and to have the hope of knowing the happiness of that glorious world above the stars."

"You must not think of that," said the old woman; "we feel ourselves to be much happier and much better off than human beings."

"So I shall die," said the little mermaid, "and as the foam of the sea I shall be driven about never again to hear the music of the waves, or to see the pretty flowers nor the red sun. Is there anything I can do to win an immortal soul?"

"No," said the old woman, "unless a man were to love you so much that you were more to him than his father or mother; and if all his thoughts and all his love were fixed upon you, and the priest placed his right hand in yours, and he promised to be true to you here and hereafter, then his soul would glide into your body and you would obtain a share in the future happiness of mankind. He would give a soul to you and retain his own as well; but this can never happen. Your fish's tail, which amongst us is considered so beautiful, is thought on earth to be quite ugly; they do not know any better, and they think it necessary to have two stout props, which they call legs, in order to be handsome."

Then the little mermaid sighed, and looked sorrowfully

at her fish's tail. "Let us be happy," said the old lady, "and dart and spring about during the three hundred years that we have to live, which is really quite long enough; after that we can rest ourselves all the better. This evening we are going to have a court ball."

It is one of those splendid sights which we can never see on earth. The walls and the ceiling of the large ball-room were of thick, but transparent crystal. Many hundreds of colossal shells, some of a deep red, others of a grass green, stood on each side in rows, with blue fire in them, which lighted up the whole saloon, and shone through the walls, so that the sea was also illuminated. Innumerable fishes, great and small, swam past the crystal walls; on some of them the scales glowed with a purple brilliancy, and on others they shone like silver and gold. Through the halls flowed a broad stream, and in it danced the mermen and the mermaids to the music of their own sweet singing. No one on earth has such a lovely voice as theirs. The little mermaid sang more sweetly than them all. The whole court applauded her with hands and tails; and for a moment her heart felt quite gay, for she knew she had the loveliest voice of any on earth or in the sea. But she soon thought again of the world above her, for she could not forget the charming prince, nor her sorrow that she had not an immortal soul like his; therefore she crept away silently out of her father's palace, and while everything within was gladness and song, she sat in her own little garden sorrowful and alone. Then she heard the bugle sounding through the water, and thought – "He is certainly sailing above, he on whom my wishes depend, and in whose hands I should like to place the happiness of my life. I will venture all for him, and to win an immortal soul, while my sisters are dancing in my father's palace, I will go to the sea witch, of whom I have always been so much afraid, but she can give me counsel and help."

And then the little mermaid went out from her garden, and took the road to the foaming whirlpools, behind which the sorceress lived. She had never been that way before: neither flowers nor grass grew there; nothing but bare, grey, sandy ground stretched out to the whirlpool, where the water, like foaming mill-wheels, whirled round everything that it seized, and cast it into the fathomless deep. Through the midst of these crushing whirlpools the little mermaid was obliged to pass, to reach the dominions of the sea witch; and also for a long distance the only road lay right across a quantity of warm, bubbling mire, called by the witch her turfmoor. Beyond this stood her house, in the centre of a strange forest, in which all the trees and flowers were polypi, half animals and half plants; they looked like serpents with a hundred heads growing out of the ground. The branches were long slimy arms, with fingers like flexible worms, moving limb after limb from the root to the top. All that could be reached in the sea they seized upon, and held fast, so that it never escaped from their clutches. The little mermaid was so alarmed at what she saw, that she stood still, and her heart beat with fear, and she was very nearly turning back; but she thought of the prince, and of the human soul for which she longed, and her courage returned. She fastened her long flowing hair round her head, so that the polypi might not seize hold of it. She laid her hands together across her bosom, and then she darted forwards as a fish shoots through the water, between the supple arms and fingers of the ugly polypi, which were stretched out on each side of her. She saw that each held in its grasp something it had seized with its numerous little arms, as if they were iron bands. The white skeletons of human beings who had perished at sea, and had sunk down into the deep waters, skeletons of land animals, oars, rudders, and chests of ships were lying tightly grasped by their clinging arms; even a little mermaid, whom they had caught and strangled; and this seemed the most shocking of all to the little princess.

She now came to a space of marshy ground in the wood, where large, fat water-snakes were rolling in the mire, and showing their ugly, drab-coloured bodies. In the midst of this spot stood a house, built with the bones of shipwrecked human beings. There sat the sea witch, allowing a toad to eat from her mouth, just as people sometimes feed a canary with a piece of sugar. She called the ugly water-snakes her little chickens, and allowed them to crawl all over her bosom.

"I know what you want," said the sea witch; "it is very stupid of you, but you shall have your way, and it will bring you to sorrow, my pretty princess. You want to get rid of your fish's tail, and to have two supports instead of it, like human beings on earth, so that the young prince may fall in love with you, and that you may have an immortal soul." And then the witch laughed so loud and disgustingly, that the toad and the snakes fell to the ground, and lay there wriggling about. "You are but just in time," said the witch; "for after sunrise to-morrow I should not be able to help you till the end of another year. I will prepare a draught for you, with which you must swim to land tomorrow before sunrise, and sit down on the shore and drink it. Your tail will then disappear, and shrink up into what mankind calls legs, and you will feel great pain, as if a sword were passing through you. But all who see you will say that you are the prettiest little human being they ever saw. You will still have the same floating gracefulness of movement, and no dancer will ever tread so lightly; but at every step you take it will feel as if you were treading upon sharp knives, and that the blood must flow. If you will bear all this, I will help you."

"Yes, I will," said the little princess in a trembling voice, as she thought of the prince and the immortal soul.

"But think again," said the witch; "for when once your shape has become like a human being, you can no more be a mermaid. You will never return through the water to your sisters, or to your father's palace again; and if you do not win the love of the prince, so that he is willing to forget his father and mother for your sake, and to love you with his whole soul, and allow the priest to join your hands that you may be man and wife, then you will never have an immortal soul.

The first morning after he marries another your heart will break, and you will become foam on the crest of the waves."

"I will do it," said the little mermaid, and she became pale as death.

"But I must be paid also," said the witch, "and it is not a trifle that I ask. You have the sweetest voice of any who dwell here in the depths of the sea, and you believe that you will be able to charm the prince with it also, but this voice you must give to me; the best thing you possess will I have for the price of my draught. My own blood must be mixed with it, that it may be as sharp as a two-edged sword."

"But if you take away my voice," said the little mermaid, "what is left for me?"

"Your beautiful form, your graceful walk, and your expressive eyes; surely with these you can enchain a man's heart. Well, have you lost your courage? Put out your little tongue that I may cut it off as my payment; then you shall have the powerful draught."

"It shall be," said the little mermaid.

Then the witch placed her cauldron on the fire, to prepare the magic draught.

"Cleanliness is a good thing," said she, scouring the vessel with snakes, which she had tied together in a large knot; then she pricked herself in the breast, and let the black blood drop into it. The steam that rose formed itself into such horrible shapes that no one could look at them without fear. Every moment the witch threw something else into the vessel, and when it began to boil, the sound was like the weeping of a crocodile. When at last the magic draught was ready, it looked like the clearest water. "There it is for you," said the witch. Then she cut off the mermaid's tongue, so that she became dumb, and would never again speak or sing. "If the polypi should seize hold of you as you return through the wood," said the witch, "throw over them a few drops of the potion, and their fingers will be torn into a thousand pieces." But the little mermaid had no occasion to do this, for the polypi sprang back in terror when they caught sight of the glittering draught, which shone in her hand like a twinkling star.

So she passed quickly through the wood and the marsh, and between the rushing whirlpools. She saw that in her father's palace the torches in the ballroom were extinguished, and all within asleep; but she did not venture to go in to them, for now she was dumb and going to leave them forever, she felt as if her heart would break. She stole into the garden, took a flower from the flower-beds of each of her sisters, kissed her hand a thousand times towards the palace, and then rose up through the dark blue waters. The sun had not risen when she came in sight of the prince's palace, and approached the beautiful marble steps, but the moon shone clear and bright. Then the little mermaid drank the magic draught, and it seemed as if a two-edged sword went through her delicate body: she fell into a swoon, and lay like one dead. When the sun arose and shone over the sea, she recovered, and felt a sharp pain; but just before her stood the handsome young prince. He fixed his coal-black eyes upon her so earnestly that she cast down her own, and then became aware that her fish's tail was gone, and that she had as pretty a pair of white legs and tiny feet as any little maiden could have; but she had no clothes, so she wrapped herself in her long, thick hair. The prince asked her who she was, and where she came from, and she looked at him mildly and sorrowfully with her deep blue eyes; but she could not speak. Every step she took was as the witch had said it would be, she felt as if treading upon the points of needles or sharp knives; but she bore it willingly, and stepped as lightly by the prince's side as a soap-bubble, so that he and all who saw her wondered at her graceful-swaying movements. She was very soon arrayed in costly robes of silk and muslin, and was the most beautiful creature in the palace; but she was dumb, and could neither speak nor sing.

Beautiful female slaves, dressed in silk and gold, stepped

forwards and sang before the prince and his royal parents: one sang better than all the others, and the prince clapped his hands and smiled at her. This was great sorrow to the little mermaid; she knew how much more sweetly she herself could sing once, and she thought, "Oh if he could only know that! I have given away my voice forever, to be with him."

The slaves next performed some pretty fairy-like dances, to the sound of beautiful music. Then the little mermaid raised her lovely white arms, stood on the tips of her toes, and glided over the floor, and danced as no one yet had been able to dance. At each moment her beauty became more revealed, and her expressive eyes appealed more directly to the heart than the songs of the slaves. Every one was enchanted, especially the prince, who called her his little foundling; and she danced again quite readily, to please him, though each time her foot touched the floor it seemed as if she trod on sharp knives.

The prince said she should remain with him always, and she received permission to sleep at his door, on a velvet cushion. He had a page's dress made for her, that she might accompany him on horseback. They rode together through the sweet-scented woods, where the green boughs touched their shoulders, and the little birds sang among the fresh leaves. She climbed with the prince to the tops of high mountains; and although her tender feet bled so that even her steps were marked, she only laughed, and followed him till they could see the clouds beneath them looking like a flock of birds travelling to distant lands. While at the prince's palace, and when all the household were asleep, she would go and sit on the broad marble steps; for it eased her burning feet to bathe them in the cold sea-water; and then she thought of all those below in the deep.

Once during the night her sisters came up arm-in-arm, singing sorrowfully, as they floated on the water. She beckoned to them, and then they recognized her, and told her how she had grieved them. After that, they came to the same place every night; and once she saw in the distance her old grandmother, who had not been to the surface of the sea for many years, and the old Sea King, her father, with his crown on his head. They stretched out their hands towards her, but they did not venture so near the land as her sisters did.

As the days passed, she loved the prince more fondly, and he loved her as he would love a little child, but it never came into his head to make her his wife; yet, unless he married her, she could not receive an immortal soul; and, on the morning after his marriage with another, she would dissolve into the foam of the sea.

"Do you not love me the best of them all?" the eyes of the little mermaid seemed to say, when he took her in his arms, and kissed her fair forehead.

"Yes, you are dear to me," said the prince; "for you have the best heart, and you are the most devoted to me; you are like a young maiden whom I once saw, but whom I shall never meet again. I was in a ship that was wrecked, and the waves cast me ashore near a holy temple, where several young maidens performed the service. The youngest of them found me on the shore, and saved my life. I saw her but twice, and she is the only one in the world whom I could love; but you are like her, and you have almost driven her image out of my mind. She belongs to the holy temple, and my good fortune has sent you to me instead of her; and we will never part."

"Ah, he knows not that it was I who saved his life," thought the little mermaid. "I carried him over the sea to the wood where the temple stands: I sat beneath the foam, and watched till the human beings came to help him. I saw the pretty maiden that he loves better than he loves me;" and the mermaid sighed deeply, but she could not shed tears. "He says the maiden belongs to the holy temple, therefore she will never return to the world. They will meet no more: while I am by his side, and see him every day. I will take care of him, and love him, and give up my life for his sake."

Very soon it was said that the prince must marry, and

that the beautiful daughter of a neighboring king would be his wife, for a fine ship was being fitted out. Although the prince gave out that he merely intended to pay a visit to the king, it was generally supposed that he really went to see his daughter. A great company were to go with him. The little mermaid smiled, and shook her head. She knew the prince's thoughts better than any of the others.

"I must travel," he had said to her; "I must see this beautiful princess; my parents desire it; but they will not oblige me to bring her home as my bride. I cannot love her; she is not like the beautiful maiden in the temple, whom you resemble. If I were forced to choose a bride, I would rather choose you, my dumb foundling, with those expressive eyes." And then he kissed her rosy mouth, played with her long waving hair, and laid his head on her heart, while she dreamed of human happiness and an immortal soul. "You are not afraid of the sea, my dumb child," said he, as they stood on the deck of the noble ship which was to carry them to the country of the neighboring king. And then he told her of storm and of calm, of strange fishes in the deep beneath them, and of what the divers had seen there; and she smiled at his descriptions, for she knew better than any one what wonders were at the bottom of the sea.

In the moonlight, when all on board were asleep, excepting the man at the helm, who was steering, she sat on the deck, gazing down through the clear water. She thought she could distinguish her father's castle, and upon it her aged grandmother, with the silver crown on her head, looking through the rushing tide at the keel of the vessel. Then her sisters came up on the waves, and gazed at her mournfully, wringing their white hands. She beckoned to them, and smiled, and wanted to tell them how happy and well off she was; but the cabin-boy approached, and when her sisters dived down he thought it was only the foam of the sea which he saw.

The next morning the ship sailed into the harbour of a beautiful town belonging to the king whom the prince was going to visit. The church bells were ringing, and from the high towers sounded a flourish of trumpets; and soldiers, with flying colours and glittering bayonets, lined the rocks through which they passed. Every day was a festival; balls and entertainments followed one another.

But the princess had not yet appeared. People said that she was being brought up and educated in a religious house, where she was learning every royal virtue. At last she came. Then the little mermaid, who was very anxious to see whether she was really beautiful, was obliged to acknowledge that she had never seen a more perfect vision of beauty. Her skin was delicately fair, and beneath her long dark eyelashes her laughing blue eyes shone with truth and purity.

"It was you," said the prince, "who saved my life when I lay dead on the beach," and he folded his blushing bride in his arms. "Oh, I am too happy," said he to the little mermaid; "my fondest hopes are all fulfilled. You will rejoice at my happiness; for your devotion to me is great and sincere."

The little mermaid kissed his hand, and felt as if her heart were already broken. His wedding morning would bring death to her, and she would change into the foam of the sea. All the church bells rung, and the heralds rode about the town proclaiming the betrothal. Perfumed oil was burning in costly silver lamps on every altar. The priests waved the censers, while the bride and bridegroom joined their hands and received the blessing of the bishop. The little mermaid, dressed in silk and gold, held up the bride's train; but her ears heard nothing of the festive music, and her eyes saw not the holy ceremony; she thought of the night of death which was coming to her, and of all she had lost in the world. On the same evening the bride and bridegroom went on board ship; cannons were roaring, flags waving, and in the centre of the ship a costly tent of purple and gold had been erected. It contained elegant couches, for the reception of the bridal pair during the night. The ship, with swelling sails and a favorable wind, glided away smoothly and lightly over the calm sea. When it grew dark a number of coloured lamps were lit, and the sailors danced merrily on the deck. The little mermaid could not help thinking of her first rising out of the sea, when she had seen similar festivities and joys; and she joined in the dance, poised herself in the air as a swallow when he pursues his prey, and all present cheered her with wonder. She had never danced so elegantly before. Her tender feet felt as if cut with sharp knives, but she cared not for it; a sharper pang had pierced through her heart. She knew this was the last evening she should ever see the prince, for whom she had forsaken her kindred and her home; she had given up her beautiful voice, and suffered unheard-of pain daily for him, while he knew nothing of it. This was the last evening that she would breathe the same air with him, or gaze on the starry sky and the deep sea; an eternal night, without a thought or a dream, awaited her: she had no soul and now she could never win one. All was joy and gayety on board ship till long after midnight; she laughed and danced with the rest, while the thoughts of death were in her heart. The prince kissed his beautiful bride, while she played with his raven hair, till they went arm-in-arm to rest in the splendid tent. Then all became still on board the ship; the helmsman, alone awake, stood at the helm. The little mermaid leaned her white arms on the edge of the vessel, and looked towards the east for the first blush of morning, for that first ray of dawn that would bring her death. She saw her sisters rising out of the flood: they were as pale as herself; but their long beautiful hair waved no more in the wind, and had been cut off.

"We have given our hair to the witch," said they, "to obtain help for you, that you may not die to-night. She has given us a knife: here it is, see it is very sharp. Before the sun rises you must plunge it into the heart of the prince; when the warm blood falls upon your feet they will grow together again, and form into a fish's tail, and you will be once more a mermaid, and return to us to live out your three hundred years before you die and change into the salt sea foam. Haste, then; he or you must die before sunrise. Our old grandmother moans so for you, that her white hair is falling off from sorrow, as ours fell under the witch's scissors. Kill the prince and come back; hasten: do you not see the first red streaks in the sky? In a few minutes the sun will rise, and you must die." And then they sighed deeply and mournfully, and sank down beneath the waves.

The little mermaid drew back the crimson curtain of the tent, and beheld the fair bride with her head resting on the prince's breast. She bent down and kissed his fair brow, then looked at the sky on which the rosy dawn grew brighter and brighter; then she glanced at the sharp knife, and again fixed her eyes on the prince, who whispered the name of his bride in his dreams. She was in his thoughts, and the knife trembled in the hand of the little mermaid: then she flung it far away from her into the waves; the water turned red where it fell, and the drops that spurted up looked like blood. She cast one more lingering, half-fainting glance at the prince, and then threw herself from the ship into the sea, and thought her body was dissolving into foam. The sun rose above the waves, and his warm rays fell on the cold foam of the little mermaid, who did not feel as if she were dying. She saw the bright sun, and all around her floated hundreds of transparent beautiful beings; she could see through them the white sails of the ship, and the red clouds in the sky; their speech was melodious, but too ethereal to be heard by mortal ears, as they were also unseen by mortal eyes. The little mermaid perceived that she had a body like theirs, and that she continued to rise higher and higher out of the foam. "Where am I?" asked she, and her voice sounded ethereal, as the voice of those who were with her; no earthly music could imitate it.

"Among the daughters of the air," answered one of them. "A mermaid has not an immortal soul, nor can she obtain one unless she wins the love of a human being. On the power of another hangs her eternal destiny. But the daughters of the air, although they do not possess an immortal soul, can, by their good deeds, procure one for themselves. We fly to warm countries, and cool the sultry air that destroys mankind with the pestilence. We carry the perfume of the flowers to spread health and restoration. After we have striven for three hundred years to all the good in our power, we receive an immortal soul and take part in the happiness of mankind. You, poor little mermaid, have tried with your whole heart to do as we are doing; you have suffered and endured and raised yourself to the spirit-world by your good deeds; and now, by striving for three hundred years in the same way, you may obtain an immortal soul."

The little mermaid lifted her glorified eyes towards the sun, and felt them, for the first time, filling with tears. On the ship, in which she had left the prince, there were life and noise; she saw him and his beautiful bride searching for her; sorrowfully they gazed at the pearly foam, as if they knew she had thrown herself into the waves. Unseen she kissed the forehead of her bride, and fanned the prince, and then mounted with the other children of the air to a rosy cloud that floated through the aether.

"After three hundred years, thus shall we float into the kingdom of heaven," said she. "And we may even get there sooner," whispered one of her companions. "Unseen we can enter the houses of men, where there are children, and for every day on which we find a good child, who is the joy of his parents and deserves their love, our time of probation is shortened. The child does not know, when we fly through the room, that we smile with joy at his good conduct, for we can count one year less of our three hundred years. But when we see a naughty or a wicked child, we shed tears of sorrow, and for every tear a day is added to our time of trial!"

LITTLE TINY, OR THUMBELINA

There was once a woman who wished very much to have a little child, but she could not obtain her wish. At last she went to a fairy, and said, "I should so very much like to have a little child; can you tell me where I can find one?"

"Oh, that can be easily managed," said the fairy. "Here is a barleycorn of a different kind to those which grow in the farmer's fields, and which the chickens eat; put it into a flower-pot, and see what will happen."

"Thank you," said the woman, and she gave the fairy twelve shillings, which was the price of the barleycorn. Then she went home and planted it, and immediately there grew up a large handsome flower, something like a tulip in appearance, but with its leaves tightly closed as if it were still a bud. "It is a beautiful flower," said the woman, and she kissed the red and golden-coloured leaves, and while she did so the flower opened, and she could see that it was a real tulip. Within the flower, upon the green velvet stamens, sat a very delicate and graceful little maiden. She was scarcely half as long as a thumb, and they gave her the name of "Thumbelina," or Tiny, because she was so small. A walnut-shell, elegantly polished, served her for a cradle; her bed was formed of blue violet-leaves, with a rose-leaf for a counterpane. Here she slept at night, but during the day she amused herself on a table, where the woman had placed a plateful of water. Round this plate were wreaths of flowers with their stems in the water, and upon it floated a large tulip-leaf, which served Tiny for a boat. Here the little maiden sat and rowed herself from side to side, with two oars made of white horse-hair. It really was a very pretty sight. Tiny could, also, sing so softly and sweetly that nothing like her singing had ever before been heard. One night, while she lay in her pretty bed, a large, ugly, wet toad crept through a broken pane of glass in the window, and leaped right upon the table where Tiny lay sleeping under her rose-leaf quilt.

"What a pretty little wife this would make for my son," said the toad, and she took up the walnut-shell in which little Tiny lay asleep, and jumped through the window with it into the garden.

In the swampy margin of a broad stream in the garden lived the toad, with her son. He was uglier even than his mother, and when he saw the pretty little maiden in her elegant bed, he could only cry, "Croak, croak, croak."

"Don't speak so loud, or she will wake," said the toad, "and then she might run away, for she is as light as swan's down. We will place her on one of the water-lily leaves out in the stream; it will be like an island to her, she is so light and small, and then she cannot escape; and, while she is away, we will make haste and prepare the state-room under the marsh, in which you are to live when you are married."

Far out in the stream grew a number of water-lilies, with broad green leaves, which seemed to float on the top of the water. The largest of these leaves appeared further off than the rest, and the old toad swam out to it with the walnut-shell, in which little Tiny lay still asleep. The tiny little creature woke very early in the morning, and began to cry bitterly when she found where she was, for she could see nothing but water on every side of the large green leaf, and no way of reaching the land. Meanwhile the old toad was very busy under the marsh, decking her room with rushes and wild yellow flowers, to make it look pretty for her new daughter-in-law. Then she swam out with her ugly son to the leaf on which she had placed poor little Tiny. She wanted to fetch the pretty bed, that she might put it in the bridal chamber to be ready for her. The old toad bowed low to her in the water, and said, "Here is my son, he will be your husband, and you will live happily in the marsh by the stream."

"Croak, croak, croak," was all her son could say for himself; so the toad took up the elegant little bed, and swam away with it, leaving Tiny all alone on the green leaf, where she sat and wept. She could not bear to think of living with the old toad, and having her ugly son for a husband. The little fishes, who swam about in the water beneath, had seen the toad, and heard what she said, so they lifted their heads above the water to look at the little maiden. As soon as they caught sight of her, they saw she was very pretty, and it made them very sorry to think that she must go and live with the ugly toads. "No, it must never be!" so they assembled together in the water, round the green stalk which held the leaf on which the little maiden stood, and gnawed it away at the root with their teeth. Then the leaf floated down the stream, carrying Tiny far away out of reach of land.

Tiny sailed past many towns, and the little birds in the bushes saw her, and sang, "What a lovely little creature;" so the leaf swam away with her further and further, till it brought her to other lands. A graceful little white butterfly constantly fluttered round her, and at last alighted on the leaf. Tiny pleased him, and she was glad of it, for now the toad could not possibly reach her, and the country through which she sailed was beautiful, and the sun shone upon the water, till it glittered like liquid gold. She took off her girdle and tied one end of it round the butterfly, and the other end of the ribbon she fastened to the leaf, which now glided on much faster than ever, taking little Tiny with it as she stood. Presently a large cockchafer flew by; the moment he caught sight of her, he seized her round her delicate waist with his claws, and flew with her into a tree. The green leaf floated away on the brook, and the butterfly flew with it, for he was fastened to it, and could not get away.

Oh, how frightened little Tiny felt when the cockchafer flew with her to the tree! But especially was she sorry for the beautiful white butterfly which she had fastened to the leaf, for if he could not free himself he would die of hunger. But the cockchafer did not trouble himself at all about the matter. He seated himself by her side on a large green leaf, gave her some honey from the flowers to eat, and told her she was very pretty, though not in the least like a cockchafer. After a time, all the cockchafers turned up their feelers, and said, "She has only two legs! how ugly that looks." "She has no feelers," said another. "Her waist is quite slim. Pooh! she is like a human being."

"Oh! she is ugly," said all the lady cockchafers, although Tiny was very pretty. Then the cockchafer who had run away with her, believed all the others when they said she was ugly, and would have nothing more to say to her, and told her she might go where she liked. Then he flew down with her from the tree, and placed her on a daisy, and she wept at the thought that she was so ugly that even the cockchafers would have nothing to say to her. And all the while she was really the loveliest creature that one could imagine, and as tender and delicate as a beautiful rose-leaf. During the whole summer poor little Tiny lived quite alone in the wide forest. She wove herself a bed with blades of grass, and hung it up under a broad leaf, to protect herself from the rain. She sucked the honey from the flowers for food, and drank the dew from their leaves every morning. So passed away the summer and the autumn, and then came the winter, – the long, cold winter. All the birds who had sung to her so sweetly were flown away, and the trees and the flowers had withered. The large clover leaf under the shelter of which she had lived, was now rolled together and shrivelled up, nothing remained but a yellow withered stalk. She felt dreadfully cold, for her clothes were torn, and she was herself so frail and delicate, that poor little Tiny was nearly frozen to death. It began to snow too; and the snow-flakes, as they fell upon her, were like a whole shovelful falling upon one of us, for we are tall, but she was only an inch high. Then she wrapped herself up in a dry leaf, but it cracked in the middle and could not keep her warm, and she shivered with cold. Near the wood in which she had been living lay a corn-field, but the corn had been cut a long time; nothing remained but the bare dry stubble standing up out of the frozen ground. It was to her like struggling through a large wood. Oh! how she shivered with the cold. She came at last to the door of a field-mouse, who had a little den under the corn-stubble. There dwelt the field-mouse in warmth and comfort, with a whole roomful of corn, a kitchen, and a beautiful dining room. Poor little Tiny stood before the door just like a little beggar-girl, and begged for a small piece of barley-corn, for she had been without a morsel to eat for two days.

"You poor little creature," said the field-mouse, who was really a good old field-mouse, "come into my warm room and dine with me." She was very pleased with Tiny, so she said, "You are quite welcome to stay with me all the winter, if you like; but you must keep my rooms clean and neat, and tell me stories, for I shall like to hear them very much." And Tiny did all the field-mouse asked her, and found herself very comfortable.

"We shall have a visitor soon," said the field-mouse one day; "my neighbour pays me a visit once a week. He is better off than I am; he has large rooms, and wears a beautiful black velvet coat. If you could only have him for a husband, you would be well provided for indeed. But he is blind, so you must tell him some of your prettiest stories."

But Tiny did not feel at all interested about this neighbour, for he was a mole. However, he came and paid his visit dressed in his black velvet coat.

"He is very rich and learned, and his house is twenty times larger than mine," said the field-mouse.

He was rich and learned, no doubt, but he always spoke slightingly of the sun and the pretty flowers, because he had never seen them. Tiny was obliged to sing to him, "Lady-bird, lady-bird, fly away home," and many other pretty songs. And the mole fell in love with her because she had such a sweet voice; but he said nothing yet, for he was very cautious. A short time before, the mole had dug a long passage under the earth, which led from the dwelling of the field-mouse to his own, and here she had permission to walk with Tiny whenever she liked. But he warned them not to be alarmed at the sight of a dead bird which lay in the passage. It was a perfect bird, with a beak and feathers, and could not have been dead long, and was lying just where the mole had made his passage. The mole took a piece of phosphorescent wood in his mouth, and it glittered like fire in the dark; then he went before them to light them through the long, dark passage. When they came to the spot where lay the dead bird, the mole pushed his broad nose through the ceiling, the earth gave way, so that there was a large hole, and the daylight shone into the passage. In the middle of the floor lay a dead swallow, his beautiful wings pulled close to his sides, his feet and his head drawn up under his feathers; the poor bird had evidently died of the cold. It made little Tiny very sad to see it, she did so love the little birds; all the summer they had sung and twittered for her so beautifully. But the mole pushed it aside with his crooked legs, and said, "He will sing no more now. How miserable it must be to be born a little bird! I am thankful that none of my children will ever be birds, for they can do nothing but cry, 'Tweet, tweet,' and always die of hunger in the winter."

"Yes, you may well say that, as a clever man!" exclaimed the field-mouse, "What is the use of his twittering, for when winter comes he must either starve or be frozen to death. Still birds are very high bred."

Tiny said nothing; but when the two others had turned their backs on the bird, she stooped down and stroked aside the soft feathers which covered the head, and kissed the closed eyelids. "Perhaps this was the one who sang to me so sweetly in the summer," she said; "and how much pleasure it gave me, you dear, pretty bird."

The mole now stopped up the hole through which the daylight shone, and then accompanied the lady home. But during the night Tiny could not sleep; so she got out of bed and wove a large, beautiful carpet of hay; then she carried it to the dead bird, and spread it over him; with some down from the flowers which she had found in the field-mouse's room. It was as soft as wool, and she spread some of it on each side of the bird, so that he might lie warmly in the cold earth. "Farewell, you pretty little bird," said she, "farewell; thank you for your delightful singing during the summer, when all the trees were green, and the warm sun shone upon us." Then she laid her head on the bird's breast, but she was alarmed immediately, for it seemed as if something inside the bird went "thump, thump." It was the bird's heart; he was not really dead, only benumbed with the cold, and the warmth had restored him to life. In autumn, all the swallows fly away into warm countries, but if one happens to linger, the cold seizes it, it becomes frozen, and falls down as if dead; it remains where it fell, and the cold snow covers it. Tiny trembled very much; she was quite frightened, for the bird was large, a great deal larger than herself, – she was only an inch high. But she took courage, laid the wool more thickly over the poor swallow, and then took a leaf which she had used for her own counterpane, and laid it over the head of the poor bird. The next morning she again stole out to see him. He was alive but very weak; he could only open his eyes for a moment to look at Tiny, who stood by holding a piece of decayed wood in her hand, for she had no other lantern. "Thank you, pretty little maiden," said the sick swallow; "I have been so nicely warmed, that I shall soon regain my strength, and be able to fly about again in the warm sunshine."

"Oh," said she, "it is cold out of doors now; it snows and freezes. Stay in your warm bed; I will take care of you."

Then she brought the swallow some water in a flower-leaf, and after he had drank, he told her that he had wounded one of his wings in a thorn-bush, and could not fly as fast as the others, who were soon far away on their journey to warm countries. Then at last he had fallen to the earth, and could remember no more, nor how he came to be where she had found him. The whole winter the swallow remained underground, and Tiny nursed him with care and love. Neither the mole nor the field-mouse knew anything about it, for they did not like swallows. Very soon the spring time came, and the sun warmed the earth. Then the swallow bade farewell to Tiny, and she opened the hole in the ceiling which the mole had made. The sun shone in upon them so beautifully, that the swallow asked her if she would go with him; she could sit on his back, he said, and he would fly away with her into the green woods. But Tiny knew it would make the field-mouse very grieved if she left her in that manner, so she said, "No, I cannot."

"Farewell, then, farewell, you good, pretty little maiden," said the swallow; and he flew out into the sunshine.

Tiny looked after him, and the tears rose in her eyes. She was very fond of the poor swallow.

"Tweet, tweet," sang the bird, as he flew out into the green woods, and Tiny felt very sad. She was not allowed to go out into the warm sunshine. The corn which had been sown in the field over the house of the field-mouse had grown up high into the air, and formed a thick wood to Tiny, who was only an inch in height.

"You are going to be married, Tiny," said the field-mouse. "My neighbour has asked for you. What good fortune for a poor child like you. Now we will prepare your wedding clothes. They must be both woollen and linen. Nothing must be wanting when you are the mole's wife."

Tiny had to turn the spindle, and the field-mouse hired four spiders, who were to weave day and night. Every evening the mole visited her, and was continually speaking of the time when the summer would be over. Then he would keep his wedding-day with Tiny; but now the heat of the sun was so great that it burned the earth, and made it quite hard, like a stone. As soon as the summer was over, the wedding should take place. But Tiny was not at all pleased; for she did not like the tiresome mole. Every morning when the sun rose, and every evening when it went down, she would creep out at the door, and as the wind blew aside the ears of corn, so that she could see the blue sky, she thought how beautiful and bright it seemed out there, and wished so much to see her dear swallow again. But he never returned; for by this time he had flown far away into the lovely green forest.

When autumn arrived, Tiny had her outfit quite ready; and the field-mouse said to her, "In four weeks the wedding must take place."

Then Tiny wept, and said she would not marry the disagreeable mole.

"Nonsense," replied the field-mouse. "Now don't be obstinate, or I shall bite you with my white teeth. He is a very handsome mole; the queen herself does not wear more beautiful velvets and furs. His kitchen and cellars are quite full. You ought to be very thankful for such good fortune."

So the wedding-day was fixed, on which the mole was to fetch Tiny away to live with him, deep under the earth, and never again to see the warm sun, because he did not like it. The poor child was very unhappy at the thought of saying farewell to the beautiful sun, and as the field-mouse had given her permission to stand at the door, she went to look at it once more.

"Farewell bright sun," she cried, stretching out her arm towards it; and then she walked a short distance from the house; for the corn had been cut, and only the dry stubble remained in the fields. "Farewell, farewell," she repeated, twining her arm round a little red flower that grew just by her side. "Greet the little swallow from me, if you should see him again."

"Tweet, tweet," sounded over her head suddenly. She looked up, and there was the swallow himself flying close by. As soon as he spied Tiny, he was delighted; and then she told him how unwilling she felt to marry the ugly mole, and to live always beneath the earth, and never to see the bright sun any more. And as she told him she wept.

"Cold winter is coming," said the swallow, "and I am going to fly away into warmer countries. Will you go with me? You can sit on my back, and fasten yourself on with your sash. Then we can fly away from the ugly mole and his gloomy rooms, – far away, over the mountains, into warmer countries, where the sun shines more brightly – than here; where it is always summer, and the flowers bloom in greater beauty. Fly now with me, dear little Tiny; you saved my life when I lay frozen in that dark passage."

"Yes, I will go with you," said Tiny; and she seated herself on the bird's back, with her feet on his outstretched wings, and tied her girdle to one of his strongest feathers.

Then the swallow rose in the air, and flew over forest and over sea, high above the highest mountains, covered with eternal snow. Tiny would have been frozen in the cold air, but she crept under the bird's warm feathers, keeping her little head uncovered, so that she might admire the beautiful lands over which they passed. At length they reached the warm countries, where the sun shines brightly, and the sky seems so much higher above the earth. Here, on the hedges, and by the wayside, grew purple, green, and white grapes; lemons and oranges hung from trees in the woods; and the air was fragrant with myrtles and orange blossoms. Beautiful children ran along the country lanes, playing with large gay butterflies; and as the swallow flew further and further, every place appeared still more lovely.

At last they came to a blue lake, and by the side of it, shaded by trees of the deepest green, stood a palace of dazzling white marble, built in the olden times. Vines clustered round its lofty pillars, and at the top were many swallows' nests, and one of these was the home of the swallow who carried Tiny.

"This is my house," said the swallow; "but it would not do for you to live there – you would not be comfortable. You must choose for yourself one of those lovely flowers, and I will put you down upon it, and then you shall have everything that you can wish to make you happy."

"That will be delightful," she said, and clapped her little hands for joy.

A large marble pillar lay on the ground, which, in falling, had been broken into three pieces. Between these pieces grew the most beautiful large white flowers; so the swallow flew down with Tiny, and placed her on one of the broad leaves. But how surprised she was to see in the middle of the flower, a tiny little man, as white and transparent as if he had been made of crystal! He had a gold crown on his head, and delicate wings at his shoulders, and was not much larger than Tiny herself. He was the angel of the flower; for a tiny man and a tiny woman dwell in every flower; and this was the king of them all.

"Oh, how beautiful he is!" whispered Tiny to the swallow.

The little prince was at first quite frightened at the bird, who was like a giant, compared to such a delicate little creature as himself; but when he saw Tiny, he was delighted, and thought her the prettiest little maiden he had ever seen. He took the gold crown from his head, and placed it on hers, and asked her name, and if she would be his wife, and queen over all the flowers.

This certainly was a very different sort of husband to the son of a toad, or the mole, with my black velvet and fur; so she said, "Yes," to the handsome prince. Then all the flowers opened, and out of each came a little lady or a tiny lord, all so pretty it was quite a pleasure to look at them. Each of them brought Tiny a present; but the best gift was a pair of beautiful wings, which had belonged to a large white fly and they fastened them to Tiny's shoulders, so that she might fly from flower to flower. Then there was much rejoicing, and the little swallow who sat above them, in his nest, was asked to sing a wedding song, which he did as well as he could; but in his heart he felt sad for he was very fond of Tiny, and would have liked never to part from her again.

"You must not be called Tiny any more," said the spirit of the flowers to her. "It is an ugly name, and you are so very pretty. We will call you Maia."

"Farewell, farewell," said the swallow, with a heavy heart as he left the warm countries to fly back into Denmark. There he had a nest over the window of a house in which dwelt the writer of fairy tales. The swallow sang, "Tweet, tweet," and from his song came the whole story.

THE PRINCESS AND THE PEA

Once upon a time there was a prince who wanted to marry a princess; but she would have to be a real princess. He travelled all over the world to find one, but nowhere could he get what he wanted. There were princesses enough, but it was difficult to find out whether they were real ones. There was always something about them that was not as it should be. So he came home again and was sad, for he would have liked very much to have a real princess.

One evening a terrible storm came on; there was thunder and lightning, and the rain poured down in torrents. Suddenly a knocking was heard at the city gate, and the old king went to open it.

It was a princess standing out there in front of the gate. But, good gracious! what a sight the rain and the wind had made her look. The water ran down from her hair and clothes; it ran down into the toes of her shoes and out again at the heels. And yet she said that she was a real princess.

"Well, we'll soon find that out," thought the old queen. But she said nothing, went into the bed-room, took all the bedding off the bedstead, and laid a pea on the bottom; then she took twenty mattresses and laid them on the pea, and then twenty eider-down beds on top of the mattresses.

On this the princess had to lie all night. In the morning she was asked how she had slept.

"Oh, very badly!" said she. "I have scarcely closed my eyes all night. Heaven only knows what was in the bed, but I was lying on something hard, so that I am black and blue all over my body. It's horrible!"

Now they knew that she was a real princess because she had felt the pea right through the twenty mattresses and the twenty eider-down beds.

Nobody but a real princess could be as sensitive as that.

So the prince took her for his wife, for now he knew that he had a real princess; and the pea was put in the museum, where it may still be seen, if no one has stolen it.

There, that is a true story.

THE RED SHOES

Once upon a time there was little girl, pretty and dainty. But in summer time she was obliged to go barefooted because she was poor, and in winter she had to wear large wooden shoes, so that her little instep grew quite red.

In the middle of the village lived an old shoemaker's wife; she sat down and made, as well as she could, a pair of little shoes out of some old pieces of red cloth. They were clumsy, but she meant well, for they were intended for the little girl, whose name was Karen.

Karen received the shoes and wore them for the first time on the day of her mother's funeral. They were certainly not suitable for mourning; but she had no others, and so she put her bare feet into them and walked behind the humble coffin.

Just then a large old carriage came by, and in it sat an old lady; she looked at the little girl, and taking pity on her, said to the clergyman, "Look here, if you will give me the little girl, I will take care of her."

Karen believed that this was all on account of the red shoes, but the old lady thought them hideous, and so they were burnt. Karen herself was dressed very neatly and cleanly; she was taught to read and to sew, and people said that she was pretty. But the mirror told her, "You are more than pretty – you are beautiful."

One day the Queen was travelling through that part of the country, and had her little daughter, who was a princess, with her. All the people, amongst them Karen too, streamed towards the castle, where the little princess, in fine white clothes, stood before the window and allowed herself to be stared at. She wore neither a train nor a golden crown, but beautiful red morocco shoes; they were indeed much finer than those which the shoemaker's wife had sewn for little Karen. There is really nothing in the world that can be compared to red shoes!

Karen was now old enough to be confirmed; she received some new clothes, and she was also to have some new shoes. The rich shoemaker in the town took the measure of her little foot in his own room, in which there stood great glass cases full of pretty shoes and white slippers. It all looked very lovely, but the old lady could not see very well, and therefore did not get much pleasure out of it. Amongst the shoes stood a pair of red ones, like those which the princess had worn. How beautiful they were! and the shoemaker said that they had been made for a count's daughter, but that they had not fitted her.

"I suppose they are of shiny leather?" asked the old lady. "They shine so."

"Yes, they do shine," said Karen. They fitted her, and were bought. But the old lady knew nothing of their being red, for she would never have allowed Karen to be confirmed in red shoes, as she was now to be.

Everybody looked at her feet, and the whole of the way from the church door to the choir it seemed to her as if even the ancient figures on the monuments, in their stiff collars and long black robes, had their eyes fixed on her red shoes. It was only of these that she thought when the clergyman laid his hand upon her head and spoke of the holy baptism, of the covenant with God, and told her that she was now to be a grown-up Christian. The organ pealed forth solemnly, and the sweet children's voices mingled with that of their old leader; but Karen thought only of her red shoes. In the afternoon the old lady heard from everybody that Karen had worn red shoes. She said that it was a shocking thing to do, that it was very improper, and that Karen was always to go to church in future in black shoes, even if they were old.

On the following Sunday there was Communion. Karen looked first at the black shoes, then at the red ones – looked at the red ones again, and put them on.

The sun was shining gloriously, so Karen and the old lady went along the footpath through the corn, where it was rather dusty.

At the church door stood an old crippled soldier leaning on a crutch; he had a wonderfully long beard, more red than white, and he bowed down to the ground and asked the old lady whether he might wipe her shoes. Then Karen put out her little foot too. "Dear me, what pretty dancing-shoes!" said the soldier. "Sit fast, when you dance," said he, addressing the shoes, and slapping the soles with his hand.

The old lady gave the soldier some money and then went with Karen into the church.

And all the people inside looked at Karen's red shoes, and all the figures gazed at them; when Karen knelt before the altar and put the golden goblet to her mouth, she thought only of the red shoes. It seemed to her as though they were swimming about in the goblet, and she forgot to sing the psalm, forgot to say the "Lord's Prayer."

Now every one came out of church, and the old lady stepped into her carriage. But just as Karen was lifting up her foot to get in too, the old soldier said: "Dear me, what pretty dancing shoes!" and Karen could not help it, she was obliged to dance a few steps; and when she had once begun, her legs continued to dance. It seemed as if the shoes had got power over them. She danced round the church corner, for she could not stop; the coachman had to run after her and seize her. He lifted her into the carriage, but her feet continued to dance, so that she kicked the good old lady violently. At last they took off her shoes, and her legs were at rest.

At home the shoes were put into the cupboard, but Karen could not help looking at them.

Now the old lady fell ill, and it was said that she would not rise from her bed again. She had to be nursed and waited upon, and this was no one's duty more than Karen's. But there was a grand ball in the town, and Karen was invited. She looked at the red shoes, saying to herself that there was no sin in doing that; she put the red shoes on, thinking there was no harm in that either; and then she went to the ball; and commenced to dance.

But when she wanted to go to the right, the shoes danced to the left, and when she wanted to dance up the room, the shoes danced down the room, down the stairs through the street, and out through the gates of the town. She danced, and was obliged to dance, far out into the dark wood. Suddenly something shone up among the trees, and she believed it was the moon, for it was a face. But it was the old soldier with the red beard; he sat there nodding his head and said: "Dear me, what pretty dancing shoes!"

She was frightened, and wanted to throw the red shoes away; but they stuck fast. She tore off her stockings, but the shoes had grown fast to her feet. She danced and was obliged to go on dancing over field and meadow, in rain and sunshine, by night and by day – but by night it was most horrible.

She danced out into the open churchyard; but the dead there did not dance. They had something better to do than that. She wanted to sit down on the pauper's grave where the bitter fern grows; but for her there was neither peace nor rest. And as she danced past the open church door she saw an angel there in long white robes, with wings reaching from his shoulders down to the earth; his face was stern and grave, and in his hand he held a broad shining sword.

"Dance you shall," said he, "dance in your red shoes till you are pale and cold, till your skin shrivels up and you are a skeleton! Dance you shall, from door to door, and where proud and wicked children live you shall knock, so that they may hear you and fear you! Dance you shall, dance—!"

"Mercy!" cried Karen. But she did not hear what the angel answered, for the shoes carried her through the gate into the fields, along highways and byways, and unceasingly she had to dance.

One morning she danced past a door that she knew well; they were singing a psalm inside, and a coffin was being carried out covered with flowers. Then she knew that she was forsaken by every one and damned by the angel of God.

She danced, and was obliged to go on dancing through the dark night. The shoes bore her away over thorns and stumps till she was all torn and bleeding; she danced away over the heath to a lonely little house. Here, she knew, lived the executioner; and she tapped with her finger at the window and said:

"Come out, come out! I cannot come in, for I must dance."

And the executioner said: "I don't suppose you know who I am. I strike off the heads of the wicked, and I notice that my axe is tingling to do so."

"Don't cut off my head!" said Karen, "for then I could not repent of my sin. But cut off my feet with the red shoes."

And then she confessed all her sin, and the executioner struck off her feet with the red shoes; but the shoes danced away with the little feet across the field into the deep forest.

And he carved her a pair of wooden feet and some crutches, and taught her a psalm which is always sung by sinners; she kissed the hand that guided the axe, and went away over the heath.

"Now, I have suffered enough for the red shoes," she said; "I will go to church, so that people can see me." And she went quickly up to the church-door; but when she came there, the red shoes were dancing before her, and she was frightened, and turned back.

During the whole week she was sad and wept many bitter tears, but when Sunday came again she said: "Now I have suffered and striven enough. I believe I am quite as good as many of those who sit in church and give themselves airs." And so she went boldly on; but she had not got further than the churchyard gate when she saw the red shoes dancing along before her. Then she became terrified, and turned back and repented right heartily of her sin.

She went to the parsonage, and begged that she might be taken into service there. She would be industrious, she said, and do everything that she could; she did not mind about the wages as long as she had a roof over her, and was with good people. The pastor's wife had pity on her, and took her into service. And she was industrious and thoughtful. She sat quiet and listened when the pastor read aloud from the Bible in the evening. All the children liked her very much, but when they spoke about dress and grandeur and beauty she would shake her head.

On the following Sunday they all went to church, and she was asked whether she wished to go too; but, with tears in her eyes, she looked sadly at her crutches. And then the others went to hear God's Word, but she went alone into her little room; this was only large enough to hold the bed and a chair. Here she sat down with her hymn-book, and as she was reading it with a pious mind, the wind carried the notes of the organ over to her from the church, and in tears she lifted up her face and said: "O God! help me!"

Then the sun shone so brightly, and right before her stood an angel of God in white robes; it was the same one whom she had seen that night at the church-door. He no longer carried the sharp sword, but a beautiful green branch, full of roses; with this he touched the ceiling, which rose up very high, and where he had touched it there shone a golden star. He touched the walls, which opened wide apart, and she saw the organ which was pealing forth; she saw the pictures of the old pastors and their wives, and the congregation sitting in the polished chairs and singing from their hymn-books. The church itself had come to the poor girl in her narrow room, or the room had gone to the church. She sat in the pew with the rest of the pastor's household, and when they had finished the hymn and looked up, they nodded and said, "It was right of you to come, Karen."

"It was mercy," said she.

The organ played and the children's voices in the choir sounded soft and lovely. The bright warm sunshine streamed through the window into the pew where Karen sat, and her heart became so filled with it, so filled with peace and joy, that it broke. Her soul flew on the sunbeams to Heaven, and no one was there who asked after the Red Shoes.

BROTHERS GRIMM

RAPUNZEL

There were once a man and a woman who had long in vain wished for a child. At length the woman hoped that God was about to grant her desire. These people had a little window at the back of their house from which a splendid garden could be seen, which was full of the most beautiful flowers and herbs. It was, however, surrounded by a high wall, and no one dared to go into it because it belonged to an enchantress, who had great power and was dreaded by all the world. One day the woman was standing by this window and looking down into the garden, when she saw a bed which was planted with the most beautiful rampion (rapunzel), and it looked so fresh and green that she longed for it, she quite pined away, and began to look pale and miserable. Then her husband was alarmed, and asked: 'What ails you, dear wife?' 'Ah,' she replied, 'if I can't eat some of the rampion, which is in the garden behind our house, I shall die.' The man, who loved her, thought: 'Sooner than let your wife die, bring her some of the rampion yourself, let it cost what it will.' At twilight, he clambered down over the wall into the garden of the enchantress, hastily clutched a handful of rampion, and took it to his wife. She at once made herself a salad of it, and ate it greedily. It tasted so good to her – so very good, that the next day she longed for it three times as much as before. If he was to have any rest, her husband must once more descend into the garden. In the gloom of evening therefore, he let himself down again; but when he had clambered down the wall he was terribly afraid, for he saw the enchantress standing before him. 'How can you dare,' said she with angry look, 'descend into my garden and steal my rampion like a thief? You shall suffer for it!' 'Ah,' answered he, 'let mercy take the place of justice, I only made up my mind to do it out of necessity. My wife saw your rampion from the window, and felt such a longing for it that she would have died if she had not got some to eat.' Then the enchantress allowed her anger to be softened, and said to him: 'If the case be as you say, I will allow you to take away with you as much rampion as you will, only I make one condition, you must give me the child which your wife will bring into the world; it shall be well treated, and I will care for it like a mother.' The man in his terror consented to everything, and when the woman was brought to bed, the enchantress appeared at once, gave the child the name of Rapunzel, and took it away with her.

Rapunzel grew into the most beautiful child under the sun. When she was twelve years old, the enchantress shut her into a tower, which lay in a forest, and had neither stairs nor door, but quite at the top was a little window. When the enchantress wanted to go in, she placed herself beneath it and cried:

> *'Rapunzel, Rapunzel,*
> *Let down your hair to me.'*

Rapunzel had magnificent long hair, fine as spun gold, and when she heard the voice of the enchantress she unfastened her braided tresses, wound them round one of the hooks of the window above, and then the hair fell twenty ells down, and the enchantress climbed up by it.

After a year or two, it came to pass that the king's son rode through the forest and passed by the tower. Then he heard a song, which was so charming that he stood still and listened. This was Rapunzel, who in her solitude passed her time in letting her sweet voice resound. The king's son wanted to climb up to her, and looked for the door of the tower, but none was to be found. He rode home, but the singing had so deeply touched his heart, that every day he went out into the forest and listened to it. Once when he was thus standing behind a tree, he saw that an enchantress came there, and he heard how she cried:

> *'Rapunzel, Rapunzel,*
> *Let down your hair to me.'*

Then Rapunzel let down the braids of her hair, and the enchantress climbed up to her. 'If that is the ladder by which one mounts, I too will try my fortune,' said he, and the next day when it began to grow dark, he went to the tower and cried:

> *'Rapunzel, Rapunzel,*
> *Let down your hair to me.'*

Immediately the hair fell down and the king's son climbed up.

At first Rapunzel was terribly frightened when a man, such as her eyes had never yet beheld, came to her; but the king's son began to talk to her quite like a friend, and told her that his heart had been so stirred that it had let him have no rest, and he had been forced to see her. Then Rapunzel lost her fear, and when he asked her if she would take him for her husband, and she saw that he was young and hand-some, she thought: 'He will love me more than old Dame Gothel does'; and she said yes, and laid her hand in his. She said: 'I will willingly go away with you, but I do not know how to get down. Bring with you a skein of silk every time that you come, and I will weave a ladder with it, and when that is ready I will descend, and you will take me on your horse.' They agreed that until that time he should come to her every evening, for the old woman came by day. The enchantress remarked nothing of this, until once Rapunzel said to her: 'Tell me, Dame Gothel, how it happens that you are so much heavier for me to draw up than the young king's son – he is with me in a moment.' 'Ah! you wicked child,' cried the enchantress. 'What do I hear you say! I thought I had separated you from all the world, and yet you have deceived me!' In her anger she clutched Rapunzel's beautiful tresses, wrapped them twice round her left hand, seized a pair of scissors with the right, and snip, snap, they were cut off, and the lovely braids lay on the ground. And she was so pitiless that she took poor Rapunzel into a desert where she had to live in great grief and misery.

On the same day that she cast out Rapunzel, however, the enchantress fastened the braids of hair, which she had cut off, to the hook of the window, and when the king's son came and cried:

> 'Rapunzel, Rapunzel,
> Let down your hair to me.'

She let the hair down. The king's son ascended, but instead of finding his dearest Rapunzel, he found the enchantress, who gazed at him with wicked and venomous looks. 'Aha!' she cried mockingly, 'you would fetch your dearest, but the beautiful bird sits no longer singing in the nest; the cat has got it, and will scratch out your eyes as well. Rapunzel is lost to you; you will never see her again.' The king's son was beside himself with pain, and in his despair he leapt down from the tower. He escaped with his life, but the thorns into which he fell pierced his eyes. Then he wandered quite blind about the forest, ate nothing but roots and berries, and did naught but lament and weep over the loss of his dearest wife. Thus he roamed about in misery for some years, and at length came to the desert where Rapunzel, with the twins to which she had given birth, a boy and a girl, lived in wretchedness. He heard a voice, and it seemed so familiar to him that he went towards it, and when he approached, Rapunzel knew him and fell on his neck and wept. Two of her tears wetted his eyes and they grew clear again, and he could see with them as before. He led her to his kingdom where he was joyfully received, and they lived for a long time afterwards, happy and contented.

HANSEL AND GRETEL

Hard by a great forest dwelt a poor wood-cutter with his wife and his two children. The boy was called Hansel and the girl Gretel. He had little to bite and to break, and once when great dearth fell on the land, he could no longer procure even daily bread. Now when he thought over this by night in his bed, and tossed about in his anxiety, he groaned and said to his wife: 'What is to become of us? How are we to feed our poor children, when we no longer have anything even for ourselves?' 'I'll tell you what, husband,' answered the woman, 'early tomorrow morning we will take the children out into the forest to where it is the thickest; there we will light a fire for them, and give each of them one more piece of bread, and then we will go to our work and leave them alone. They will not find the way home again, and we shall be rid of them.' 'No, wife,' said the man, 'I will not do that; how can I bear to leave my children alone in the forest? – the wild animals would soon come and tear them to pieces.' 'O, you fool!' said she, 'then we must all four die of hunger, you may as well plane the planks for our coffins,' and she left him no peace until he consented. 'But I feel very sorry for the poor children, all the same,' said the man.

The two children had also not been able to sleep for

hunger, and had heard what their stepmother had said to their father. Gretel wept bitter tears, and said to Hansel: 'Now all is over with us.' 'Be quiet, Gretel,' said Hansel, 'do not distress yourself, I will soon find a way to help us.' And when the old folks had fallen asleep, he got up, put on his little coat, opened the door below, and crept outside. The moon shone brightly, and the white pebbles which lay in front of the house glittered like real silver pennies. Hansel stooped and stuffed the little pocket of his coat with as many as he could get in. Then he went back and said to Gretel: 'Be comforted, dear little sister, and sleep in peace, God will not forsake us,' and he lay down again in his bed. When day dawned, but before the sun had risen, the woman came and awoke the two children, saying: 'Get up, you sluggards! we are going into the forest to fetch wood.' She gave each a little piece of bread, and said: 'There is something for your dinner, but do not eat it up before then, for you will get nothing else.' Gretel took the bread under her apron, as Hansel had the pebbles in his pocket. Then they all set out together on the way to the forest. When they had walked a short time, Hansel stood still and peeped back at the house, and did so again and again. His father said: 'Hansel, what are you looking at there and staying behind for? Pay attention, and do not forget how to use your legs.' 'Ah, father,' said Hansel, 'I am looking at my little white cat, which is sitting up on the roof, and wants to say goodbye to me.' The wife said: 'Fool, that is not your little cat, that is the morning sun which is shining on the chimneys.' Hansel, however, had not been looking back at the cat, but had been constantly throwing one of the white pebble-stones out of his pocket on the road.

When they had reached the middle of the forest, the father said: 'Now, children, pile up some wood, and I will light a fire that you may not be cold.' Hansel and Gretel gathered brushwood together, as high as a little hill. The brushwood was lighted, and when the flames were burning very high, the woman said: 'Now, children, lay yourselves down by the fire and rest, we will go into the forest and cut some wood. When we have done, we will come back and fetch you away.' Hansel and Gretel sat by the fire, and when noon came, each ate a little piece of bread, and as they heard the strokes of the wood-axe they believed that their father was near. It was not the axe, however, but a branch which he had fastened to a withered tree which the wind was blowing backwards and forwards. And as they had been sitting such a long time, their eyes closed with fatigue, and they fell fast asleep. When at last they awoke, it was already dark night. Gretel began to cry and said: 'How are we to get out of the forest now?' But Hansel comforted her and said: 'Just wait a little, until the moon has risen, and then we will soon find the way.' And when the full moon had risen, Hansel took his little sister by the hand, and followed the pebbles which shone like newly-coined silver pieces, and showed them the way.

They walked the whole night long, and by break of day came once more to their father's house. They knocked at the door, and when the woman opened it and saw that it was Hansel and Gretel, she said: 'You naughty children, why have you slept so long in the forest? – we thought you were never coming back at all!' The father, however, rejoiced, for it had cut him to the heart to leave them behind alone.

Not long afterwards, there was once more great dearth throughout the land, and the children heard their mother saying at night to their father: 'Everything is eaten again, we have one half loaf left, and that is the end. The children must go, we will take them farther into the wood, so that they will not find their way out again; there is no other means of saving ourselves!' The man's heart was heavy, and he thought: 'It would be better for you to share the last mouthful with your children.' The woman, however, would listen to nothing that he had to say, but scolded and reproached him. He who says

A must say B, likewise, and as he had yielded the first time, he had to do so a second time also.

The children, however, were still awake and had heard the conversation. When the old folks were asleep, Hansel again got up, and wanted to go out and pick up pebbles as he had done before, but the woman had locked the door, and Hansel could not get out. Nevertheless he comforted his little sister, and said: 'Do not cry, Gretel, go to sleep quietly, the good God will help us.'

Early in the morning came the woman, and took the children out of their beds. Their piece of bread was given to them, but it was still smaller than the time before. On the way into the forest Hansel crumbled his in his pocket, and often stood still and threw a morsel on the ground. 'Hansel, why do you stop and look round?' said the father, 'go on.' 'I am looking back at my little pigeon which is sitting on the roof, and wants to say goodbye to me,' answered Hansel. 'Fool!' said the woman, 'that is not your little pigeon, that is the morning sun that is shining on the chimney.' Hansel, however little by little, threw all the crumbs on the path.

The woman led the children still deeper into the forest, where they had never in their lives been before. Then a great fire was again made, and the mother said: 'Just sit there, you children, and when you are tired you may sleep a little; we are going into the forest to cut wood, and in the evening when we are done, we will come and fetch you away.' When it was noon, Gretel shared her piece of bread with Hansel, who had scattered his by the way. Then they fell asleep and evening passed, but no one came to the poor children. They did not awake until it was dark night, and Hansel comforted his little sister and said: 'Just wait, Gretel, until the moon rises, and then we shall see the crumbs of bread which I have strewn about, they will show us our way home again.' When the moon came they set out, but they found no crumbs, for the many thousands of birds which fly about in the woods and fields had picked them all up. Hansel said to Gretel: 'We shall soon find the way,' but they did not find it. They walked the whole night and all the next day too from morning till evening, but they did not get out of the forest, and were very hungry, for they had nothing to eat but two or three berries, which grew on the ground. And as they were so weary that their legs would carry them no longer, they lay down beneath a tree and fell asleep.

It was now three mornings since they had left their father's house. They began to walk again, but they always came deeper into the forest, and if help did not come soon, they must die of hunger and weariness. When it was mid-day, they saw a beautiful snow-white bird sitting on a bough, which sang so delightfully that they stood still and listened to it. And when its song was over, it spread its wings and flew away before them, and they followed it until they reached a little house, on the roof of which it alighted; and when they approached the little house they saw that it was built of bread and covered with cakes, but that the windows were of clear sugar. 'We will set to work on that,' said Hansel, 'and have a good meal. I will eat a bit of the roof, and you Gretel, can eat some of the window, it will taste sweet.' Hansel reached up above, and broke off a little of the roof to try how it tasted, and Gretel leant against the window and nibbled at the panes. Then a soft voice cried from the parlour:

> 'Nibble, nibble, gnaw,
> Who is nibbling at my little house?'

The children answered:

> 'The wind, the wind,
> The heaven-born wind,'

and went on eating without disturbing themselves. Hansel, who liked the taste of the roof, tore down a great piece of it, and Gretel pushed out the whole of one round window-pane, sat down, and enjoyed herself with it. Suddenly the door opened, and a woman as old as the hills, who supported herself on crutches, came creeping out. Hansel and Gretel were so terribly frightened that they let fall what they had in their hands. The old woman, however, nodded her head, and said: 'Oh, you dear children, who has brought you here? do come in, and stay with me. No harm shall happen to you.' She took them both by the hand, and led them into her little house. Then good food was set before them, milk and pancakes, with sugar, apples, and nuts. Afterwards two pretty little beds were covered with clean white linen, and Hansel and Gretel lay down in them, and thought they were in heaven.

The old woman had only pretended to be so kind; she was in reality a wicked witch, who lay in wait for children, and had only built the little house of bread in order to entice them there. When a child fell into her power, she killed it, cooked and ate it, and that was a feast day with her. Witches have red eyes, and cannot see far, but they have a keen scent like the beasts, and are aware when human beings draw near. When Hansel and Gretel came into her neighbourhood, she laughed with malice, and said mockingly: 'I have them, they shall not escape me again!' Early in the morning before the children were awake, she was already up, and when she saw both of them sleeping and looking so pretty, with their plump and rosy cheeks she muttered to herself: 'That will be a dainty mouthful!' Then she seized Hansel with her shrivelled hand, carried him into a little stable, and locked him in behind a grated door. Scream as he might, it would not help him. Then she went to Gretel, shook her till she awoke, and cried: 'Get up, lazy thing, fetch some water, and cook something good for your brother, he is in the stable outside, and is to be made fat. When he is fat, I will eat him.' Gretel began to weep bitterly, but it was all in vain, for she was forced to do what the wicked witch commanded.

And now the best food was cooked for poor Hansel, but Gretel got nothing but crab-shells. Every morning the woman crept to the little stable, and cried: 'Hansel, stretch out your finger that I may feel if you will soon be fat.' Hansel, however, stretched out a little bone to her, and the old woman, who had dim eyes, could not see it, and thought it was Hansel's finger, and was astonished that there was no way of fattening him. When four weeks had gone by, and Hansel still remained thin, she was seized with impatience and would not wait any longer. 'Now, then, Gretel,' she cried to the girl, 'stir yourself, and bring some water. Let Hansel be fat or lean, tomorrow I will kill him, and cook him.' Ah, how the poor little sister did lament when she had to fetch the water, and how her tears did flow down her cheeks! 'Dear God, do help us,' she cried. 'If the wild beasts in the forest had but devoured us, we should at any rate have died together.' 'Just keep your noise to yourself,' said the old woman, 'it won't help you at all.'

Early in the morning, Gretel had to go out and hang up the cauldron with the water, and light the fire. 'We will bake first,' said the old woman, 'I have already heated the oven, and kneaded the dough.' She pushed poor Gretel out to the oven, from which flames of fire were already darting. 'Creep in,' said the witch, 'and see if it is properly heated, so that we can put the bread in.' And once Gretel was inside, she intended to shut the oven and let her bake in it, and then she would eat her, too. But Gretel saw what she had in mind, and said: 'I do not know how I am to do it; how do I get in?' 'Silly goose,' said the old woman. 'The door is big enough; just look, I can get in myself!' and she crept up and thrust her head into the oven. Then Gretel gave her a push that drove her far into it, and shut the iron door, and fastened the bolt. Oh! then she began to howl quite horribly, but Gretel ran away and the godless witch was miserably burnt to death.

Gretel, however, ran like lightning to Hansel, opened his little stable, and cried: 'Hansel, we are saved! The old witch is dead!' Then Hansel sprang like a bird from its cage when the door is opened. How they did rejoice and embrace each other, and dance about and kiss each other! And as they had no longer any need to fear her, they went into the witch's house, and in every corner there stood chests full of pearls and jewels. 'These are far better than pebbles!' said Hansel, and thrust into his pockets whatever could be got in, and Gretel said: 'I, too, will take something home with me,' and filled her pinafore full. 'But now we must be off,' said Hansel, 'that we may get out of the witch's forest.'

When they had walked for two hours, they came to a great stretch of water. 'We cannot cross,' said Hansel, 'I see no foot-plank, and no bridge.' 'And there is also no ferry,' answered Gretel, 'but a white duck is swimming there: if I ask her, she will help us over.' Then she cried:

> 'Little duck, little duck, dost thou see,
> Hansel and Gretel are waiting for thee?
> There's never a plank, or bridge in sight,
> Take us across on thy back so white.'

The duck came to them, and Hansel seated himself on its back, and told his sister to sit by him. 'No,' replied Gretel, 'that will be too heavy for the little duck; she shall take us across, one after the other.' The good little duck did so, and when they were once safely across and had walked for a short time, the forest seemed to be more and more familiar to them, and at length they saw from afar their father's house. Then they began to run, rushed into the parlour, and threw themselves round their father's neck. The man had not known one happy hour since he had left the children in the forest; the woman, however, was dead. Gretel emptied her pinafore until pearls and precious stones ran about the room, and

Hansel threw one handful after another out of his pocket to add to them. Then all anxiety was at an end, and they lived together in perfect happiness. My tale is done, there runs a mouse; whosoever catches it, may make himself a big fur cap out of it.

LITTLE RED-CAP, OR
LITTLE RED RIDING HOOD

Once upon a time there was a dear little girl who was loved
by everyone who looked at her, but most of all by her grandmother, and there was nothing that she would not have given
to the child. Once she gave her a little cap of red velvet, which
suited her so well that she would never wear anything else;
so she was always called 'Little Red-Cap.'

One day her mother said to her: 'Come, Little Red-Cap,
here is a piece of cake and a bottle of wine; take them to your
grandmother, she is ill and weak, and they will do her good.
Set out before it gets hot, and when you are going, walk nicely
and quietly and do not run off the path, or you may fall and
break the bottle, and then your grandmother will get nothing;
and when you go into her room, don't forget to say, "Good
morning", and don't peep into every corner before you do it.'

'I will take great care,' said Little Red-Cap to her mother,
and gave her hand on it.

The grandmother lived out in the wood, half a league
from the village, and just as Little Red-Cap entered the wood,
a wolf met her. Red-Cap did not know what a wicked creature
he was, and was not at all afraid of him.

'Good day, Little Red-Cap,' said he.

'Thank you kindly, wolf.'

'Whither away so early, Little Red-Cap?'

'To my grandmother's.'

'What have you got in your apron?'

'Cake and wine; yesterday was baking-day, so poor sick grandmother is to have something good, to make her stronger.'

'Where does your grandmother live, Little Red-Cap?'

'A good quarter of a league farther on in the wood; her house stands under the three large oak-trees, the nut-trees are just below; you surely must know it,' replied Little Red-Cap.

The wolf thought to himself: 'What a tender young creature! what a nice plump mouthful – she will be better to eat than the old woman. I must act craftily, so as to catch both.' So he walked for a short time by the side of Little Red-Cap, and then he said: 'See, Little Red-Cap, how pretty the flowers are about here – why do you not look round? I believe, too, that you do not hear how sweetly the little birds are singing; you walk gravely along as if you were going to school, while everything else out here in the wood is merry.'

Little Red-Cap raised her eyes, and when she saw the sunbeams dancing here and there through the trees, and pretty flowers growing everywhere, she thought: 'Suppose I take grandmother a fresh nosegay; that would please her too. It is so early in the day that I shall still get there in good time'; and so she ran from the path into the wood to look for flowers. And whenever she had picked one, she fancied that she saw a still prettier one farther on, and ran after it, and so got deeper and deeper into the wood.

Meanwhile the wolf ran straight to the grandmother's house and knocked at the door.

'Who is there?'

'Little Red-Cap,' replied the wolf. 'She is bringing cake and wine; open the door.'

'Lift the latch,' called out the grandmother, 'I am too weak, and cannot get up.'

The wolf lifted the latch, the door sprang open, and without saying a word he went straight to the grandmother's bed, and devoured her. Then he put on her clothes, dressed himself in her cap laid himself in bed and drew the curtains.

Little Red-Cap, however, had been running about picking flowers, and when she had gathered so many that she could carry no more, she remembered her grandmother, and set out on the way to her.

She was surprised to find the cottage-door standing open, and when she went into the room, she had such a strange feeling that she said to herself: 'Oh dear! how uneasy I feel today, and at other times I like being with grandmother so much.' She called out: 'Good morning,' but received no answer; so she went to the bed and drew back the curtains. There lay her grandmother with her cap pulled far over her face, and looking very strange.

'Oh! grandmother,' she said, 'what big ears you have!'

'The better to hear you with, my child,' was the reply.

'But, grandmother, what big eyes you have!' she said.

'The better to see you with, my dear.'

'But, grandmother, what large hands you have!'

'The better to hug you with.'

'Oh! but, grandmother, what a terrible big mouth you have!'

'The better to eat you with!'

And scarcely had the wolf said this, than with one bound he was out of bed and swallowed up Red-Cap.

When the wolf had appeased his appetite, he lay down again in the bed, fell asleep and began to snore very loud. The huntsman was just passing the house, and thought to himself: 'How the old woman is snoring! I must just see if she wants anything.' So he went into the room, and when he came to the bed, he saw that the wolf was lying in it. 'Do I find you here, you old sinner!' said he. 'I have long sought you!' Then just as he was going to fire at him, it occurred to him that the wolf might have devoured the grandmother, and that she might still be saved, so he did not fire, but took a pair of scissors, and began to cut open the stomach of the sleeping wolf. When he had made two snips, he saw the little Red-Cap shining, and then he made two snips more, and the little girl sprang out, crying: 'Ah, how frightened I have been! How dark it was inside the wolf; and after that the aged grandmother came out alive also, but scarcely able to breathe. Red-Cap, however, quickly fetched great stones with which they filled the wolf's belly, and when he awoke, he wanted to run away, but the stones were so heavy that he collapsed at once, and fell dead.

Then all three were delighted. The huntsman drew off the wolf's skin and went home with it; the grandmother ate the cake and drank the wine which Red-Cap had brought, and revived, but Red-Cap thought to herself: 'As long as I live, I will never by myself leave the path, to run into the wood, when my mother has forbidden me to do so.'

It also related that once when Red-Cap was again taking cakes to the old grandmother, another wolf spoke to her, and tried to entice her from the path. Red-Cap, however, was on her guard, and went straight forward on her way, and told her grandmother that she had met the wolf, and that he had said 'good morning' to her, but with such a wicked look in his eyes, that if they had not been on the public road she was certain he would have eaten her up. 'Well,' said the grandmother, 'we will shut the door, that he may not come in.' Soon afterwards the wolf knocked, and cried: 'Open the door, grandmother, I am Little Red-Cap, and am bringing you some cakes.' But they did not speak, or open the door, so the greybeard stole twice or thrice round the house, and at last jumped on the roof, intending to wait until Red-Cap went home in the evening, and then to steal after her and devour her in the darkness. But the grandmother saw what was in his thoughts. In front of the house was a great stone trough, so she said to the child: 'Take the pail, Red-Cap; I made some sausages yesterday, so carry the water in which I boiled them to the trough.' Red-Cap carried until the great trough was quite full. Then the smell of the sausages reached the wolf, and he sniffed and peeped down, and at last stretched out his neck so far that he could no longer keep his footing and began to slip, and slipped down from the roof straight into the great trough, and was drowned. But Red-Cap went joyously home, and no one ever did anything to harm her again.

THE ELVES AND THE SHOEMAKER

There was once a shoemaker, who worked very hard and was very honest: but still he could not earn enough to live upon; and at last all he had in the world was gone, save just leather enough to make one pair of shoes.

Then he cut his leather out, all ready to make up the next day, meaning to rise early in the morning to his work. His conscience was clear and his heart light amidst all his troubles; so he went peaceably to bed, left all his cares to Heaven, and soon fell asleep. In the morning after he had said his prayers, he sat himself down to his work; when, to his great wonder, there stood the shoes all ready made, upon the table. The good man knew not what to say or think at such an odd thing happening. He looked at the workmanship; there was not one false stitch in the whole job; all was so neat and true, that it was quite a masterpiece.

The same day a customer came in, and the shoes suited him so well that he willingly paid a price higher than usual for them; and the poor shoemaker, with the money, bought leather enough to make two pairs more. In the evening he cut out the work, and went to bed early, that he might get up and begin betimes next day; but he was saved all the trouble, for when he got up in the morning the work was done ready to his hand. Soon in came buyers, who paid him handsomely for his goods, so that he bought leather enough for four pair more. He cut out the work again overnight and found it done in the morning, as before; and so it went on for some time: what was got ready in the evening was always done by daybreak, and the good man soon became thriving and well off again.

One evening, about Christmas-time, as he and his wife were sitting over the fire chatting together, he said to her, 'I should like to sit up and watch tonight, that we may see who it is that comes and does my work for me.' The wife liked the thought; so they left a light burning, and hid themselves in a corner of the room, behind a curtain that was hung up there, and watched what would happen.

As soon as it was midnight, there came in two little naked dwarfs; and they sat themselves upon the shoemaker's bench, took up all the work that was cut out, and began to ply with their little fingers, stitching and rapping and tapping away at such a rate, that the shoemaker was all wonder, and could not take his eyes off them. And on they went, till the job was quite done, and the shoes stood ready for use upon the table. This was long before daybreak; and then they bustled away as quick as lightning.

The next day the wife said to the shoemaker. 'These little wights have made us rich, and we ought to be thankful to them, and do them a good turn if we can. I am quite sorry to see them run about as they do; and indeed it is not very decent, for they have nothing upon their backs to keep off the cold. I'll tell you what, I will make each of them a shirt, and a coat and waistcoat, and a pair of pantaloons into the bargain; and do you make each of them a little pair of shoes.'

The thought pleased the good cobbler very much; and one evening, when all the things were ready, they laid them on the table, instead of the work that they used to cut out, and then went and hid themselves, to watch what the little elves would do.

About midnight in they came, dancing and skipping, hopped round the room, and then went to sit down to their work as usual; but when they saw the clothes lying for them, they laughed and chuckled, and seemed mightily delighted.

Then they dressed themselves in the twinkling of an eye, and danced and capered and sprang about, as merry as could be; till at last they danced out at the door, and away over the green.

The good couple saw them no more; but everything went well with them from that time forward, as long as they lived.

SNOW-WHITE AND ROSE-RED

There was once a poor widow who lived in a lonely cottage. In front of the cottage was a garden wherein stood two rose-trees, one of which bore white and the other red roses. She had two children who were like the two rose-trees, and one was called Snow-white, and the other Rose-red. They were as good and happy, as busy and cheerful as ever two children in the world were, only Snow-white was more quiet and gentle than Rose-red. Rose-red liked better to run about in the meadows and fields seeking flowers and catching butterflies; but Snow-white sat at home with her mother, and helped her with her housework, or read to her when there was nothing to do.

The two children were so fond of one another that they always held each other by the hand when they went out together, and when Snow-white said: 'We will not leave each other,' Rose-red answered: 'Never so long as we live,' and their mother would add: 'What one has she must share with the other.'

They often ran about the forest alone and gathered red berries, and no beasts did them any harm, but came close to them trustfully. The little hare would eat a cabbage-leaf out of their hands, the roe grazed by their side, the stag leapt merrily by them, and the birds sat still upon the boughs, and sang whatever they knew.

No mishap overtook them; if they had stayed too late in the forest, and night came on, they laid themselves down near one another upon the moss, and slept until morning came, and their mother knew this and did not worry on their account.

Once when they had spent the night in the wood and the dawn had roused them, they saw a beautiful child in a shining white dress sitting near their bed. He got up and looked quite kindly at them, but said nothing and went into the forest. And when they looked round they found that they had been sleeping quite close to a precipice, and would certainly have fallen into it in the darkness if they had gone only a few paces further. And their mother told them that it must have been the angel who watches over good children.

Snow-white and Rose-red kept their mother's little cottage so neat that it was a pleasure to look inside it. In the summer Rose-red took care of the house, and every morning laid a wreath of flowers by her mother's bed before she awoke, in which was a rose from each tree. In the winter Snow-white lit the fire and hung the kettle on the hob. The kettle was of brass and shone like gold, so brightly was it polished. In the evening, when the snowflakes fell, the mother said: 'Go, Snow-white, and bolt the door,' and then they sat round the hearth, and the mother took her spectacles and read aloud out of a large book, and the two girls listened as they sat and spun. And close by them lay a lamb upon the floor, and behind them upon a perch sat a white dove with its head hidden beneath its wings.

One evening, as they were thus sitting comfortably together, someone knocked at the door as if he wished to be let in. The mother said: 'Quick, Rose-red, open the door, it must be a traveller who is seeking shelter.' Rose-red went and pushed back the bolt, thinking that it was a poor man, but it was not; it was a bear that stretched his broad, black head within the door.

Rose-red screamed and sprang back, the lamb bleated, the dove fluttered, and Snow-white hid herself behind her mother's bed. But the bear began to speak and said: 'Do not be afraid, I will do you no harm! I am half-frozen, and only want to warm myself a little beside you.'

'Poor bear,' said the mother, 'lie down by the fire, only take care that you do not burn your coat.' Then she cried: 'Snow-white, Rose-red, come out, the bear will do you no harm, he means well.' So they both came out, and by-and-by the lamb and dove came nearer, and were not afraid of him. The bear said: 'Here, children, knock the snow out of my coat a little'; so they brought the broom and swept the bear's hide clean; and he stretched himself by the fire and growled contentedly and comfortably. It was not long before they grew quite at home, and played tricks with their clumsy guest. They tugged his hair with their hands, put their feet upon his back and rolled him about, or they took a hazel-switch and beat him, and when he growled they laughed. But the bear took it all in good part, only when they were too rough he called out: 'Leave me alive, children,

> 'Snow-white, Rose-red,
> Will you beat your wooer dead?'

When it was bed-time, and the others went to bed, the mother said to the bear: 'You can lie there by the hearth, and then you will be safe from the cold and the bad weather.' As soon as day dawned the two children let him out, and he trotted across the snow into the forest.

Henceforth the bear came every evening at the same time, laid himself down by the hearth, and let the children amuse themselves with him as much as they liked; and they got so used to him that the doors were never fastened until their black friend had arrived.

When spring had come and all outside was green, the bear said one morning to Snow-white: 'Now I must go away, and cannot come back for the whole summer.' 'Where are you going, then, dear bear?' asked Snow-white. 'I must go into the forest and guard my treasures from the wicked dwarfs. In the winter, when the earth is frozen hard, they are obliged to stay below and cannot work their way through; but now, when the sun has thawed and warmed the earth, they break through it, and come out to pry and steal; and what once gets into their hands, and in their caves, does not easily see daylight again.'

Snow-white was quite sorry at his departure, and as she unbolted the door for him, and the bear was hurrying out, he caught against the bolt and a piece of his hairy coat was torn off, and it seemed to Snow-white as if she had seen gold shining through it, but she was not sure about it. The bear ran away quickly, and was soon out of sight behind the trees.

A short time afterwards the mother sent her children into the forest to get firewood. There they found a big tree which lay felled on the ground, and close by the trunk something was jumping backwards and forwards in the grass, but they could not make out what it was. When they came nearer they saw a dwarf with an old withered face and a snow-white beard a yard long. The end of the beard was caught in a crevice of the tree, and the little fellow was jumping about like a dog tied to a rope, and did not know what to do.

He glared at the girls with his fiery red eyes and cried: 'Why do you stand there? Can you not come here and help me?' 'What are you up to, little man?' asked Rose-red. 'You stupid, prying goose!' answered the dwarf: 'I was going to split the tree to get a little wood for cooking. The little bit of food that we people get is immediately burnt up with heavy logs; we do not swallow so much as you coarse, greedy folk.

I had just driven the wedge safely in, and everything was going as I wished; but the cursed wedge was too smooth and suddenly sprang out, and the tree closed so quickly that I could not pull out my beautiful white beard; so now it is tight and I cannot get away, and the silly, sleek, milk-faced things laugh! Ugh! how odious you are!'

The children tried very hard, but they could not pull the beard out, it was caught too fast. 'I will run and fetch someone,' said Rose-red. 'You senseless goose!' snarled the dwarf; 'why should you fetch someone? You are already two too many for me; can you not think of something better?' 'Don't be impatient,' said Snow-white, 'I will help you,' and she pulled her scissors out of her pocket, and cut off the end of the beard.

As soon as the dwarf felt himself free he laid hold of a bag which lay amongst the roots of the tree, and which was full of gold, and lifted it up, grumbling to himself: 'Uncouth people, to cut off a piece of my fine beard. Bad luck to you!' and then he swung the bag upon his back, and went off without even once looking at the children.

Some time afterwards Snow-white and Rose-red went to catch a dish of fish. As they came near the brook they saw something like a large grasshopper jumping towards the water, as if it were going to leap in. They ran to it and found it was the dwarf. 'Where are you going?' said Rose-red; 'you surely don't want to go into the water?' 'I am not such a fool!' cried the dwarf; 'don't you see that the accursed fish wants to pull me in?' The little man had been sitting there fishing, and unluckily the wind had tangled up his beard with the fishing-line; a moment later a big fish made a bite and the feeble creature had not strength to pull it out; the fish kept the upper hand and pulled the dwarf towards him. He held on to all the reeds and rushes, but it was of little good, for he was forced to follow the movements of the fish, and was in urgent danger of being dragged into the water.

The girls came just in time; they held him fast and tried to free his beard from the line, but all in vain, beard and line were entangled fast together. There was nothing to do but to bring out the scissors and cut the beard, whereby a small part of it was lost. When the dwarf saw that he screamed out: 'Is that civil, you toadstool, to disfigure a man's face? Was it not enough to clip off the end of my beard? Now you have cut off the best part of it. I cannot let myself be seen by my people. I wish you had been made to run the soles off your shoes!' Then he took out a sack of pearls which lay in the rushes, and without another word he dragged it away and disappeared behind a stone.

It happened that soon afterwards the mother sent the two children to the town to buy needles and thread, and laces and ribbons. The road led them across a heath upon which huge pieces of rock lay strewn about. There they noticed a large bird hovering in the air, flying slowly round and round above them; it sank lower and lower, and at last settled near a rock not far away. Immediately they heard a loud, piteous cry. They ran up and saw with horror that the eagle had seized their old acquaintance the dwarf, and was going to carry him off.

The children, full of pity, at once took tight hold of the little man, and pulled against the eagle so long that at last he let his booty go. As soon as the dwarf had recovered from his first fright he cried with his shrill voice: 'Could you not have done it more carefully! You dragged at my brown coat so that it is all torn and full of holes, you clumsy creatures!' Then he took up a sack full of precious stones, and slipped away again under the rock into his hole. The girls, who by this time were used to his ingratitude, went on their way and did their business in town.

As they crossed the heath again on their way home they surprised the dwarf, who had emptied out his bag of precious stones in a clean spot, and had not thought that anyone would come there so late. The evening sun shone upon the brilliant stones; they glittered and sparkled with all colours so beautifully that the children stood still and stared at them. 'Why do you stand gaping there?' cried the dwarf, and his ashengrey face became copper-red with rage. He was still cursing when a loud growling was heard, and a black bear came trotting towards them out of the forest. The dwarf sprang up in a fright, but he could not reach his cave, for the bear was already close. Then in the dread of his heart he cried: 'Dear Mr Bear, spare me, I will give you all my treasures; look, the beautiful jewels lying there! Grant me my life; what do you want with such a slender little fellow as I? you would not feel me between your teeth. Come, take these two wicked girls, they are tender morsels for you, fat as young quails; for mercy's sake eat them!' The bear took no heed of his words, but gave the wicked creature a single blow with his paw, and he did not move again.

The girls had run away, but the bear called to them: 'Snow-white and Rose-red, do not be afraid; wait, I will come with you.' Then they recognized his voice and waited, and when he came up to them suddenly his bearskin fell off, and he stood there a handsome man, clothed all in gold. 'I am a king's son,' he said, 'and I was bewitched by that wicked dwarf, who had stolen my treasures; I have had to run about the forest as a savage bear until I was freed by his death. Now he has got his well-deserved punishment.

Snow-white was married to him, and Rose-red to his brother, and they divided between them the great treasure which the dwarf had gathered together in his cave. The old mother lived peacefully and happily with her children for many years. She took the two rose-trees with her, and they stood before her window, and every year bore the most beautiful roses, white and red.

CHARLES PERRAULT

BLUE BEARD

Once upon a time there was a man who owned splendid town and country houses, gold and silver plate, tapestries and coaches gilt all over. But the poor fellow had a blue beard, and this made him so ugly and frightful that there was not a woman or girl who did not run away at sight of him.

Amongst his neighbours was a lady of high degree who had two surpassingly beautiful daughters. He asked for the hand of one of these in marriage, leaving it to their mother to choose which should be bestowed upon him. Both girls, however, raised objections, and his offer was bandied from one to the other, neither being able to bring herself to accept a man with a blue beard. Another reason for their distaste was the fact that he had already married several wives, and no one knew what had become of them.

In order that they might become better acquainted, Blue Beard invited the two girls, with their mother and three or four of their best friends, to meet a party of young men from the neighbourhood at one of his country houses. Here they spent eight whole days, and throughout their stay there was a constant round of picnics, hunting and fishing expeditions, dances, dinners, and luncheons; and they never slept at all, through spending all the night in playing merry pranks upon each other. In short, everything went so gaily that the younger daughter began to think the master of the house had not so very blue a beard after all, and that he was an exceedingly agreeable man. As soon as the party returned to town their marriage took place.

At the end of a month Blue Beard informed his wife that important business obliged him to make a journey into a distant part of the country, which would occupy at least six weeks. He begged her to amuse herself well during his absence, and suggested that she should invite some of her friends and take them, if she liked, to the country. He was particularly anxious that she should enjoy herself thoroughly.

'Here,' he said, 'are the keys of the two large storerooms, and here is the one that locks up the gold and silver plate which is not in everyday use. This key belongs to the strong-boxes where my gold and silver is kept, this to the caskets containing my jewels; while here you have the master-key which gives admittance to all the apartments. As regards this little key, it is the key of the small room at the end of the long passage on the lower floor. You may open everything, you may go everywhere, but I forbid you to enter this little room. And I forbid you so seriously that if you were indeed to open the door, I should be so angry that I might do anything.'

She promised to follow out these instructions exactly, and after embracing her, Blue Beard steps into his coach and is off upon his journey.

Her neighbours and friends did not wait to be invited before coming to call upon the young bride, so great was their eagerness to see the splendours of her house. They had not dared to venture while her husband was there, for his blue beard frightened them. But in less than no time there they were, running in and out of the rooms, the closets, and the wardrobes, each of which was finer than the last. Presently they went upstairs to the storerooms, and there they could not admire enough the profusion and magnificence of the tapestries, beds, sofas, cabinets, tables, and stands. There were mirrors in which they could view themselves from top to toe, some with frames of plate glass, others with frames of silver and gilt lacquer, that were the most superb and beautiful things that had ever been seen. They were loud and persistent in their envy of their friend's good fortune. She, on the other hand, derived little amusement from the sight of all these riches, the reason being that she was impatient to go and inspect the little room on the lower floor.

So overcome with curiosity was she that, without reflecting upon the discourtesy of leaving her guests, she ran down a private staircase, so precipitately that twice or thrice she nearly broke her neck, and so reached the door of the little room. There she paused for a while, thinking of the prohibition which her husband had made, and reflecting that harm might come to her as a result of disobedience. But the temptation was so great that she could not conquer it. Taking the little key, with a trembling hand she opened the door of the room.

At first she saw nothing, for the windows were closed, but after a few moments she perceived dimly that the floor was entirely covered with clotted blood, and that in this were reflected the dead bodies of several women that hung along the walls. These were all the wives of Blue Beard, whose throats he had cut, one after another.

She thought to die of terror, and the key of the room, which she had just withdrawn from the lock, fell from her hand.

When she had somewhat regained her senses, she picked up the key, closed the door, and went up to her chamber to compose herself a little. But this she could not do, for her nerves were too shaken. Noticing that the key of the little room was stained with blood, she wiped it two or three times. But the blood did not go. She washed it well, and even rubbed it with sand and grit. Always the blood remained. For the key was bewitched, and there was no means of cleaning it completely. When the blood was removed from one side, it reappeared on the other.

Blue Beard returned from his journey that very evening. He had received some letters on the way, he said, from which he learned that the business upon which he had set forth had just been concluded to his satisfaction. His wife did everything she could to make it appear that she was delighted by his speedy return.

On the morrow he demanded the keys. She gave them to him, but with so trembling a hand that he guessed at once what had happened.

'How comes it,' he said to her, 'that the key of the little room is not with the others?'

'I must have left it upstairs upon my table.' she said.

'Do not fail to bring it to me presently.' said Blue Beard.

After several delays the key had to be brought. Blue Beard examined it, and addressed his wife.

'Why is there blood on this key?'

'I do not know at all,' replied the poor woman, paler than death.

'You do not know at all?' exclaimed Blue Beard; 'I know well enough. You wanted to enter the little room! Well, madam, enter it you shall – you shall go and take your place among the ladies you have seen there.'

She threw herself at her husband's feet, asking his pardon with tears, and with all the signs of a true repentance for her disobedience. She would have softened a rock, in her beauty and distress, but Blue Beard had a heart harder than any stone.

'You must die, madam,' he said; 'and at once.'

'Since I must die.' she replied, gazing at him with eyes that were wet with tears, 'give me a little time to say my prayers.'

'I give you one quarter of an hour,' replied Blue Beard, 'but not a moment longer.'

When the poor girl was alone, she called her sister to her and said:

'Sister Anne' – for that was her name – 'go up, I implore you, to the top of the tower, and see if my brothers are not approaching. They promised that they would come and visit me to-day. If you see them, make signs to them to hasten.'

Sister Anne went up to the top of the tower, and the poor unhappy girl cried out to her from time to time:

'Anne, Sister Anne, do you see nothing coming?'

And Sister Anne replied:

'I see nought but dust in the sun and the green grass growing.'

Presently Blue Beard, grasping a great cutlass, cried out at the top of his voice:

'Come down quickly, or I shall come upstairs myself.'

'Oh please, one moment more.' called out his wife.

And at the same moment she cried in a whisper:

'Anne, Sister Anne, do you see nothing coming?'

'I see nought but dust in the sun and the green grass growing.'

'Come down at once, I say.' shouted Blue Beard, 'or I will come upstairs myself.'

'I am coming.' replied his wife.

Then she called:

'Anne, Sister Anne, do you see nothing coming?'

'I see,' replied Sister Anne, 'a great cloud of dust which comes this way.'

'Is it my brothers?'

'Alas, sister, no; it is but a flock of sheep.'

'Do you refuse to come down?' roared Blue Beard.

'One little moment more!' exclaimed his wife.

Once more she cried:

'Anne, Sister Anne, do you see nothing coming?'

'I see,' replied her sister, 'two horsemen who come this way, but they are as yet a long way off . . . Heaven be praised!'

she exclaimed a moment later, 'they are my brothers . . . I am signalling to them all I can to hasten.'

Blue Beard let forth so mighty a shout that the whole house shook. The poor wife went down and cast herself at his feet, all dishevelled and in tears.

'That avails you nothing,' said Blue Beard; 'you must die.'

Seizing her by the hair with one hand, and with the other brandishing the cutlass aloft, he made as if to cut off her head.

The poor woman, turning towards him and fixing a dying gaze upon him, begged for a brief moment in which to collect her thoughts.

'No! no!' he cried; 'commend your soul to Heaven.' And raising his arm—

At this very moment there came so loud a knocking at the gate that Blue Beard stopped short. The gate was opened, and two horsemen dashed in, who drew their swords and rode straight at Blue Beard. The latter recognised them as the brothers of his wife – one of them a dragoon, and the other a musketeer – and fled instantly in an effort to escape. But the two brothers were so close upon him that they caught him ere he could gain the first flight of steps. They plunged their swords through his body and left him dead. The poor woman was nearly as dead as her husband, and had not the strength to rise and embrace her brothers.

It was found that Blue Beard had no heirs, and that consequently his wife became mistress of all his wealth. She devoted a portion to arranging a marriage between her sister Anne and a young gentleman with whom the latter had been for some time in love, while another portion purchased a captain's commission for each of her brothers. The rest formed a dowry for her own marriage with a very worthy man, who banished from her mind all memory of the evil days she had spent with Blue Beard.

CINDERELLA, OR THE LITTLE GLASS SLIPPER

Once upon a time there was a worthy man who married for his second wife the haughtiest, proudest woman that had ever been seen. She had two daughters, who possessed their mother's temper and resembled her in everything. Her husband, on the other hand, had a young daughter, who was of an exceptionally sweet and gentle nature. She got this from her mother, who had been the nicest person in the world.

The wedding was no sooner over than the stepmother began to display her bad temper. She could not endure the excellent qualities of this young girl, for they made her own daughters appear more hateful than ever. She thrust upon her all the meanest tasks about the house. It was she who had to clean the plates and the stairs, and sweep out the rooms of the mistress of the house and her daughters. She slept on a wretched mattress in a garret at the top of the house, while the sisters had rooms with parquet flooring, and beds of the most fashionable style, with mirrors in which they could see themselves from top to toe.

The poor girl endured everything patiently, not daring to complain to her father. The latter would have scolded her, because he was entirely ruled by his wife. When she had finished her work she used to sit amongst the cinders in the corner of the chimney, and it was from this habit that she came to be commonly known as Cindertail. The younger of the two sisters, who was not quite so spiteful as the elder, called her Cinderella. But her wretched clothes did not prevent Cinderella from being a hundred times more beautiful than her sisters, for all their resplendent garments.

It happened that the king's son gave a ball, and he invited all persons of high degree. The two young ladies were invited amongst others, for they cut a considerable figure in the country. Not a little pleased were they, and the question of what clothes and what mode of dressing the hair would become them best took up all their time. And all this meant fresh trouble for Cinderella, for it was she who went over her sisters' linen and ironed their ruffles. They could talk of nothing else but the fashions in clothes.

'For my part,' said the elder, 'I shall wear my dress of red velvet, with the Honiton lace.'

'I have only my everyday petticoat,' said the younger, 'but to make up for it I shall wear my cloak with the golden flowers and my necklace of diamonds, which are not so bad.'

They sent for a good hairdresser to arrange their double-frilled caps, and bought patches at the best shop.

They summoned Cinderella and asked her advice, for she had good taste. Cinderella gave them the best possible suggestions, and even offered to dress their hair, to which they gladly agreed.

While she was thus occupied they said:

'Cinderella, would you not like to go to the ball?'

'Ah, but you fine young ladies are laughing at me. It would be no place for me.'

'That is very true, people would laugh to see a cindertail in the ballroom.'

Any one else but Cinderella would have done their hair amiss, but she was good-natured, and she finished them off to perfection. They were so excited in their glee that for nearly two days they ate nothing. They broke more than a dozen laces through drawing their stays tight in order to make their waists more slender, and they were perpetually in front of a mirror.

At last the happy day arrived. Away they went, Cinderella watching them as long as she could keep them in sight. When she could no longer see them she began to cry. Her godmother found her in tears, and asked what was troubling her.

'I should like – I should like–'

She was crying so bitterly that she could not finish the sentence.

Said her godmother, who was a fairy:

'You would like to go to the ball, would you not?'

'Ah, yes,' said Cinderella, sighing.

'Well, well,' said her godmother, 'promise to be a good girl and I will arrange for you to go.'

She took Cinderella into her room and said:

'Go into the garden and bring me a pumpkin.'

Cinderella went at once and gathered the finest that she could find. This she brought to her godmother, wondering how a pumpkin could help in taking her to the ball.

Her godmother scooped it out, and when only the rind was left, struck it with her wand. Instantly the pumpkin was changed into a beautiful coach, gilded all over.

Then she went and looked in the mouse-trap, where she found six mice all alive. She told Cinderella to lift the door of the mouse-trap a little, and as each mouse came out she gave it a tap with her wand, whereupon it was transformed into a fine horse. So that here was a fine team of six dappled mouse-grey horses.

But she was puzzled to know how to provide a coachman.

'I will go and see,' said Cinderella, 'if there is not a rat in the rat-trap. We could make a coachman of him.'

'Quite right,' said her godmother, 'go and see.'

Cinderella brought in the rat-trap, which contained three big rats. The fairy chose one specially on account of his elegant whiskers.

As soon as she had touched him he turned into a fat coachman with the finest moustachios that ever were seen.

'Now go into the garden and bring me the six lizards which you will find behind the water-butt.'

No sooner had they been brought than the godmother turned them into six lackeys, who at once climbed up behind the coach in their braided liveries, and hung on there as if they had never done anything else all their lives.

Then said the fairy godmother:

'Well, there you have the means of going to the ball. Are you satisfied?'

'Oh, yes, but am I to go like this in my ugly clothes?'

Her godmother merely touched her with her wand, and on the instant her clothes were changed into garments of gold and silver cloth, bedecked with jewels. After that her godmother gave her a pair of glass slippers, the prettiest in the world.

Thus altered, she entered the coach. Her godmother bade her not to stay beyond midnight whatever happened, warning her that if she remained at the ball a moment longer, her coach would again become a pumpkin, her horses mice, and her lackeys lizards, while her old clothes would reappear upon her once more.

She promised her godmother that she would not fail to leave the ball before midnight, and away she went, beside herself with delight.

The king's son, when he was told of the arrival of a great princess whom nobody knew, went forth to receive her. He handed her down from the coach, and led her into the hall where the company was assembled. At once there fell a great silence. The dancers stopped, the violins played no more, so rapt was the attention which everybody bestowed upon the superb beauty of the unknown guest. Everywhere could be heard in confused whispers:

'Oh, how beautiful she is!'

The king, old man as he was, could not take his eyes off her, and whispered to the queen that it was many a long day since he had seen any one so beautiful and charming.

All the ladies were eager to scrutinise her clothes and the dressing of her hair, being determined to copy them on the morrow, provided they could find materials so fine, and tailors so clever.

The king's son placed her in the seat of honour, and at once begged the privilege of being her partner in a dance. Such was the grace with which she danced that the admiration of all was increased.

A magnificent supper was served, but the young prince could eat nothing, so taken up was he with watching her. She went and sat beside her sisters, and bestowed numberless attentions upon them. She made them share with her the oranges and lemons which the king had given her – greatly to their astonishment, for they did not recognise her.

While they were talking, Cinderella heard the clock strike a quarter to twelve. She at once made a profound curtsey to the company, and departed as quickly as she could.

As soon as she was home again she sought out her godmother, and having thanked her, declared that she wished to go upon the morrow once more to the ball, because the king's son had invited her.

While she was busy telling her godmother all that had happened at the ball, her two sisters knocked at the door. Cinderella let them in.

'What a long time you have been in coming!' she declared, rubbing her eyes and stretching herself as if she had only just awakened. In real truth she had not for a moment wished to sleep since they had left.

'If you had been at the ball,' said one of the sisters, 'you would not be feeling weary. There came a most beautiful princess, the most beautiful that has ever been seen, and she bestowed numberless attentions upon us, and gave us her oranges and lemons.'

Cinderella was overjoyed. She asked them the name of the princess, but they replied that no one knew it, and that the king's son was so distressed that he would give anything in the world to know who she was.

Cinderella smiled, and said she must have been beautiful indeed.

'Oh, how lucky you are. Could I not manage to see her? Oh, please, Javotte, lend me the yellow dress which you wear every day.'

'Indeed!' said Javotte, 'that is a fine idea. Lend my dress to a grubby cindertail like you – you must think me mad!'

Cinderella had expected this refusal. She was in no way upset, for she would have been very greatly embarrassed had her sister been willing to lend the dress.

The next day the two sisters went to the ball, and so did Cinderella, even more splendidly attired than the first time.

The king's son was always at her elbow, and paid her endless compliments.

The young girl enjoyed herself so much that she forgot her godmother's bidding completely, and when the first stroke of midnight fell upon her ears, she thought it was no more than eleven o'clock.

She rose and fled as nimbly as a fawn. The prince followed her, but could not catch her. She let fall one of her glass slippers, however, and this the prince picked up with tender care.

When Cinderella reached home she was out of breath, without coach, without lackeys, and in her shabby clothes. Nothing remained of all her splendid clothes save one of the little slippers, the fellow to the one which she had let fall.

Inquiries were made of the palace doorkeepers as to whether they had seen a princess go out, but they declared they had seen no one leave except a young girl, very ill-clad, who looked more like a peasant than a young lady.

When her two sisters returned from the ball, Cinderella asked them if they had again enjoyed themselves, and if the beautiful lady had been there. They told her that she was present, but had fled away when midnight sounded, and in such haste that she had let fall one of her little glass slippers, the prettiest thing in the world. They added that the king's son, who picked it up, had done nothing but gaze at it for the rest of the ball, from which it was plain that he was deeply in love with its beautiful owner.

They spoke the truth. A few days later, the king's son caused a proclamation to be made by trumpeters, that he would take for wife the owner of the foot which the slipper would fit.

They tried it first on the princesses, then on the duchesses and the whole of the Court, but in vain. Presently they brought it to the home of the two sisters, who did all they could to squeeze a foot into the slipper. This, however, they could not manage.

Cinderella was looking on and recognised her slipper:

'Let me see,' she cried, laughingly, 'if it will not fit me.'

Her sisters burst out laughing, and began to gibe at her, but the equerry who was trying on the slipper looked closely at Cinderella. Observing that she was very beautiful he declared that the claim was quite a fair one, and that his orders were to try the slipper on every maiden. He bade Cinderella sit down, and on putting the slipper to her little foot he perceived that the latter slid in without trouble, and was moulded to its shape like wax.

Great was the astonishment of the two sisters at this, and greater still when Cinderella drew from her pocket the other little slipper. This she likewise drew on.

At that very moment her godmother appeared on the scene. She gave a tap with her wand to Cinderella's clothes, and transformed them into a dress even more magnificent than her previous ones.

The two sisters recognised her for the beautiful person whom they had seen at the ball, and threw themselves at her feet, begging her pardon for all the ill-treatment she had suffered at their hands.

Cinderella raised them, and declaring as she embraced them that she pardoned them with all her heart, bade them to love her well in future.

She was taken to the palace of the young prince in all her new array. He found her more beautiful than ever, and was married to her a few days afterwards.

Cinderella was as good as she was beautiful. She set aside apartments in the palace for her two sisters, and married them the very same day to two gentlemen of high rank about the Court.

THE SLEEPING BEAUTY
IN THE WOOD

Once upon a time there lived a king and queen who were grieved, more grieved than words can tell, because they had no children. They tried the waters of every country, made vows and pilgrimages, and did everything that could be done, but without result. At last, however, the queen found that her wishes were fulfilled, and in due course she gave birth to a daughter.

A grand christening was held, and all the fairies that could be found in the realm (they numbered seven in all) were invited to be godmothers to the little princess. This was done so that by means of the gifts which each in turn would bestow upon her (in accordance with the fairy custom of those days) the princess might be endowed with every imaginable perfection.

When the christening ceremony was over, all the company returned to the king's palace, where a great banquet was held in honour of the fairies. Places were laid for them in magnificent style, and before each was placed a solid gold casket containing a spoon, fork, and knife of fine gold, set with diamonds and rubies. But just as all were sitting down to table an aged fairy was seen to enter, whom no one had thought to invite – the reason being that for more than fifty years she had never quitted the tower in which she lived, and people had supposed her to be dead or bewitched.

By the king's orders a place was laid for her, but it was impossible to give her a golden casket like the others, for only seven had been made for the seven fairies. The old creature believed that she was intentionally slighted, and muttered threats between her teeth.

She was overheard by one of the young fairies, who was seated near by. The latter, guessing that some mischievous gift might be bestowed upon the little princess, hid behind the tapestry as soon as the company left the table. Her intention was to be the last to speak, and so to have the power of counteracting, as far as possible, any evil which the old fairy might do.

Presently the fairies began to bestow their gifts upon the princess. The youngest ordained that she should be the most beautiful person in the world; the next, that she should have the temper of an angel; the third, that she should do everything with wonderful grace; the fourth, that she should dance to perfection; the fifth, that she should sing like a nightingale; and the sixth, that she should play every kind of music with the utmost skill.

It was now the turn of the aged fairy. Shaking her head, in token of spite rather than of infirmity, she declared that the princess should prick her hand with a spindle, and die of it. A shudder ran through the company at this terrible gift. All eyes were filled with tears.

But at this moment the young fairy stepped forth from behind the tapestry.

'Take comfort, your Majesties,' she cried in a loud voice; 'your daughter shall not die. My power, it is true, is not enough to undo all that my aged kinswoman has decreed: the princess will indeed prick her hand with a spindle. But instead of dying she shall merely fall into a profound slumber that will last a hundred years. At the end of that time a king's son shall come to awaken her.'

The king, in an attempt to avert the unhappy doom pronounced by the old fairy, at once published an edict forbidding all persons, under pain of death, to use a spinning-wheel or keep a spindle in the house.

At the end of fifteen or sixteen years the king and queen happened one day to be away, on pleasure bent. The princess was running about the castle, and going upstairs from room to room she came at length to a garret at the top of a tower, where an old serving-woman sat alone with her distaff, spinning. This good woman had never heard speak of the king's proclamation forbidding the use of spinning-wheels.

'What are you doing, my good woman?' asked the princess.

'I am spinning, my pretty child,' replied the dame, not knowing who she was.

'Oh, what fun!' rejoined the princess; 'how do you do it? Let me try and see if I can do it equally well.'

Partly because she was too hasty, partly because she was a little heedless, but also because the fairy decree had ordained it, no sooner had she seized the spindle than she pricked her hand and fell down in a swoon.

In great alarm the good dame cried out for help. People came running from every quarter to the princess. They threw water on her face, chafed her with their hands, and rubbed her temples with the royal essence of Hungary. But nothing would restore her.

Then the king, who had been brought upstairs by the commotion, remembered the fairy prophecy. Feeling certain that what had happened was inevitable, since the fairies had decreed it, he gave orders that the princess should be placed in the finest apartment in the palace, upon a bed embroidered in gold and silver.

You would have thought her an angel, so fair was she to

behold. The trance had not taken away the lovely colour of her complexion. Her cheeks were delicately flushed, her lips like coral. Her eyes, indeed, were closed, but her gentle breathing could be heard, and it was therefore plain that she was not dead. The king commanded that she should be left to sleep in peace until the hour of her awakening should come.

When the accident happened to the princess, the good fairy who had saved her life by condemning her to sleep a hundred years was in the kingdom of Mataquin, twelve thousand leagues away. She was instantly warned of it, however, by a little dwarf who had a pair of seven-league boots, which are boots that enable one to cover seven leagues at a single step. The fairy set off at once, and within an hour her chariot of fire, drawn by dragons, was seen approaching.

The king handed her down from her chariot, and she approved of all that he had done. But being gifted with great powers of foresight, she bethought herself that when the princess came to be awakened, she would be much distressed to find herself all alone in the old castle. And this is what she did.

She touched with her wand everybody (except the king and queen) who was in the castle – governesses, maids of honour, ladies-in-waiting, gentlemen, officers, stewards, cooks, scullions, errand boys, guards, porters, pages, footmen. She touched likewise all the horses in the stables, with their grooms, the big mastiffs in the courtyard, and little Puff, the pet dog of the princess, who was lying on the bed beside his mistress. The moment she had touched them they all fell asleep, to awaken only at the same moment as their mistress. Thus they would always be ready with their service whenever she should require it. The very spits before the fire, loaded with partridges and pheasants, subsided into slumber, and the fire as well. All was done in a moment, for the fairies do not take long over their work.

Then the king and queen kissed their dear child, without

waking her, and left the castle. Proclamations were issued, forbidding any approach to it, but these warnings were not needed, for within a quarter of an hour there grew up all round the park so vast a quantity of trees big and small, with interlacing brambles and thorns, that neither man nor beast could penetrate them. The tops alone of the castle towers could be seen, and these only from a distance. Thus did the fairy's magic contrive that the princess, during all the time of her slumber, should have nought whatever to fear from prying eyes.

At the end of a hundred years the throne had passed to another family from that of the sleeping princess. One day the king's son chanced to go a-hunting that way, and seeing in the distance some towers in the midst of a large and dense forest, he asked what they were. His attendants told him in reply the various stories which they had heard. Some said there was an old castle haunted by ghosts, others that all the witches of the neighbourhood held their revels there. The favourite tale was that in the castle lived an ogre, who carried thither all the children whom he could catch. There he devoured them at his leisure, and since he was the only person who could force a passage through the wood nobody had been able to pursue him.

While the prince was wondering what to believe, an old peasant took up the tale.

'Your Highness.' said he, 'more than fifty years ago I heard my father say that in this castle lies a princess, the most beautiful that has ever been seen. It is her doom to sleep there for a hundred years, and then to be awakened by a king's son, for whose coming she waits.'

This story fired the young prince. He jumped immediately to the conclusion that it was for him to see so gay an adventure through, and impelled alike by the wish for love and glory, he resolved to set about it on the spot.

Hardly had he taken a step towards the wood when the

tall trees, the brambles and the thorns, separated of themselves and made a path for him. He turned in the direction of the castle, and espied it at the end of a long avenue. This avenue he entered, and was surprised to notice that the trees closed up again as soon as he had passed, so that none of his retinue were able to follow him. A young and gallant prince is always brave, however; so he continued on his way, and presently reached a large fore-court.

The sight that now met his gaze was enough to fill him with an icy fear. The silence of the place was dreadful, and death seemed all about him. The recumbent figures of men and animals had all the appearance of being lifeless, until he perceived by the pimply noses and ruddy faces of the porters that they merely slept. It was plain, too, from their glasses, in which were still some dregs of wine, that they had fallen asleep while drinking.

The prince made his way into a great courtyard, paved with marble, and mounting the staircase entered the guard-room. Here the guards were lined up on either side in two ranks, their muskets on their shoulders, snoring their hardest. Through several apartments crowded with ladies and gentlemen in waiting, some seated, some standing, but all asleep, he pushed on, and so came at last to a chamber which was decked all over with gold. There he encountered the most beautiful sight he had ever seen. Reclining upon a bed, the curtains of which on every side were drawn back, was a princess of seemingly some fifteen or sixteen summers, whose radiant beauty had an almost unearthly lustre.

Trembling in his admiration he drew near and went on his knees beside her. At the same moment, the hour of disenchantment having come, the princess awoke, and bestowed upon him a look more tender than a first glance might seem to warrant.

'Is it you, dear prince?' she said; 'you have been long in coming!'

Charmed by these words, and especially by the manner in which they were said, the prince scarcely knew how to express his delight and gratification. He declared that he loved her better than he loved himself. His words were faltering, but they pleased the more for that. The less there is of eloquence, the more there is of love.

Her embarrassment was less than his, and that is not to be wondered at, since she had had time to think of what she would say to him. It seems (although the story says nothing about it) that the good fairy had beguiled her long slumber with pleasant dreams. To be brief, after four hours of talking they had not succeeded in uttering one half of the things they had to say to each other.

Now the whole palace had awakened with the princess. Every one went about his business, and since they were not all in love they presently began to feel mortally hungry. The lady-in-waiting, who was suffering like the rest, at length lost patience, and in a loud voice called out to the princess that supper was served.

The princess was already fully dressed, and in most magnificent style. As he helped her to rise, the prince refrained from telling her that her clothes, with the straight collar which she wore, were like those to which his grandmother had been accustomed. And in truth, they in no way detracted from her beauty.

They passed into an apartment hung with mirrors, and were there served with supper by the stewards of the household, while the fiddles and oboes played some old music – and played it remarkably well, considering they had not played at all for just upon a hundred years. A little later, when supper was over, the chaplain married them in the castle chapel, and in due course, attended by the courtiers in waiting, they retired to rest.

They slept but little, however. The princess, indeed, had not much need of sleep, and as soon as morning came the prince took his leave of her. He returned to the city, and told his father, who was awaiting him with some anxiety, that he had lost himself while hunting in the forest, but had obtained some black bread and cheese from a charcoal-burner, in whose hovel he had passed the night. His royal father, being of an easy-going nature, believed the tale, but his mother was not so easily hoodwinked. She noticed that he now went hunting every day, and that he always had an excuse handy when he had slept two or three nights from home. She felt certain, therefore, that he had some love affair.

Two whole years passed since the marriage of the prince and princess, and during that time they had two children. The first, a daughter, was called 'Dawn' while the second, a boy, was named 'Day' because he seemed even more beautiful than his sister.

Many a time the queen told her son that he ought to settle down in life. She tried in this way to make him confide in her, but he did not dare to trust her with his secret. Despite the affection which he bore her, he was afraid of his mother, for she came of a race of ogres, and the king had only married her for her wealth.

It was whispered at the Court that she had ogrish instincts, and that when little children were near her she had the greatest difficulty in the world to keep herself from pouncing on them.

No wonder the prince was reluctant to say a word.

But at the end of two years the king died, and the prince found himself on the throne. He then made public announcement of his marriage, and went in state to fetch his royal consort from her castle. With her two children beside her she made a triumphal entry into the capital of her husband's realm.

Some time afterwards the king declared war on his neighbour, the Emperor Cantalabutte. He appointed the queen-mother as regent in his absence, and entrusted his wife and children to her care.

He expected to be away at the war for the whole of the summer, and as soon as he was gone the queen-mother sent her daughter-in-law and the two children to a country mansion in the forest. This she did that she might be able the more easily to gratify her horrible longings. A few days later she went there herself, and in the evening summoned the chief steward.

'For my dinner to-morrow,' she told him, 'I will eat little Dawn.'

'Oh, Madam!' exclaimed the steward.

'That is my will,' said the queen; and she spoke in the tones of an ogre who longs for raw meat.

'You will serve her with piquant sauce,' she added.

The poor man, seeing plainly that it was useless to trifle with an ogress, took his big knife and went up to little Dawn's chamber. She was at that time four years old, and when she came running with a smile to greet him, flinging her arms round his neck and coaxing him to give her some sweets, he burst into tears, and let the knife fall from his hand.

Presently he went down to the yard behind the house, and slaughtered a young lamb. For this he made so delicious a sauce that his mistress declared she had never eaten anything so good.

At the same time the steward carried little Dawn to his wife, and bade the latter hide her in the quarters which they had below the yard.

Eight days later the wicked queen summoned her steward again.

'For my supper,' she announced, 'I will eat little Day.'

The steward made no answer, being determined to trick her as he had done previously. He went in search of little Day, whom he found with a tiny foil in his hand, making brave passes – though he was but three years old – at a big monkey. He carried him off to his wife, who stowed him away in hiding with little Dawn. To the ogress the steward served up, in place of Day, a young kid so tender that she found it surpassingly delicious.

So far, so good. But there came an evening when this evil queen again addressed the steward.

'I have a mind,' she said, 'to eat the queen with the same sauce as you served with her children.'

This time the poor steward despaired of being able to practise another deception. The young queen was twenty years old, without counting the hundred years she had been asleep. Her skin, though white and beautiful, had become a little tough, and what animal could he possibly find that would correspond to her? He made up his mind that if he would save his own life he must kill the queen, and went upstairs to her apartment determined to do the deed once and for all. Goading himself into a rage he drew his knife and entered the young queen's chamber, but a reluctance to give her no moment of grace made him repeat respectfully the command which he had received from the queen-mother.

'Do it! do it!' she cried, baring her neck to him; 'carry out the order you have been given! Then once more I shall see my children, my poor children that I loved so much!'

Nothing had been said to her when the children were stolen away, and she believed them to be dead.

The poor steward was overcome by compassion. 'No, no, Madam.' he declared; 'you shall not die, but you shall certainly see your children again. That will be in my quarters, where I have hidden them. I shall make the queen eat a young hind in place of you, and thus trick her once more.'

Without more ado he led her to his quarters, and leaving her there to embrace and weep over her children, proceeded to cook a hind with such art that the queen-mother ate it for her supper with as much appetite as if it had indeed been the young queen.

The queen-mother felt well satisfied with her cruel deeds, and planned to tell the king, on his return, that savage wolves had devoured his consort and his children. It was her habit, however, to prowl often about the courts and alleys of the mansion, in the hope of scenting raw meat, and one evening she heard the little boy Day crying in a basement cellar. The child was weeping because his mother had threatened to whip him for some naughtiness, and she heard at the same time the voice of Dawn begging forgiveness for her brother.

The ogress recognised the voices of the queen and her children, and was enraged to find she had been tricked. The next morning, in tones so affrighting that all trembled, she ordered a huge vat to be brought into the middle of the courtyard. This she filled with vipers and toads, with snakes and serpents of every kind, intending to cast into it the queen and her children, and the steward with his wife and serving-girl. By her command these were brought forward, with their hands tied behind their backs.

There they were, and her minions were making ready to cast them into the vat, when into the courtyard rode the king! Nobody had expected him so soon, but he had travelled post-haste. Filled with amazement, he demanded to know what this horrible spectacle meant. None dared tell him, and at that moment the ogress, enraged at what confronted her, threw herself head foremost into the vat, and was devoured on the instant by the hideous creatures she had placed in it.

The king could not but be sorry, for after all she was his mother; but it was not long before he found ample consolation in his beautiful wife and children.

PUSS IN BOOTS

A certain miller had three sons, and when he died the sole worldly goods which he bequeathed to them were his mill, his ass, and his cat. This little legacy was very quickly divided up, and you may be quite sure that neither notary nor attorney were called in to help, for they would speedily have grabbed it all for themselves.

The eldest son took the mill, and the second son took the ass. Consequently all that remained for the youngest son was the cat, and he was not a little disappointed at receiving such a miserable portion.

'My brothers,' said he, 'will be able to get a decent living by joining forces, but for my part, as soon as I have eaten my cat and made a muff out of his skin, I am bound to die of hunger.'

These remarks were overheard by Puss, who pretended not to have been listening, and said very soberly and seriously:

'There is not the least need for you to worry, Master. All you have to do is to give me a pouch, and get a pair of boots made for me so that I can walk in the woods. You will find then that your share is not so bad after all.'

Now this cat had often shown himself capable of performing cunning tricks. When catching rats and mice, for example, he would hide himself amongst the meal and hang downwards by the feet as though he were dead. His master, therefore, though he did not build too much on what the cat had said, felt some hope of being assisted in his miserable plight.

On receiving the boots which he had asked for, Puss gaily pulled them on. Then he hung the pouch round his neck, and holding the cords which tied it in front of him with his paws, he sallied forth to a warren where rabbits abounded. Placing some bran and lettuce in the pouch, he stretched himself out and lay as if dead. His plan was to wait until some young rabbit, unlearned in worldly wisdom, should come and rummage in the pouch for the eatables which he had placed there.

Hardly had he laid himself down when things fell out as he wished. A stupid young rabbit went into the pouch, and Master Puss, pulling the cords tight, killed him on the instant.

Well satisfied with his capture, Puss departed to the king's palace. There he demanded an audience, and was ushered upstairs. He entered the royal apartment, and bowed profoundly to the king.

'I bring you, Sire.' said he, 'a rabbit from the warren of the marquis of Carabas (such was the title he invented for his master), which I am bidden to present to you on his behalf.'

'Tell your master,' replied the king, 'that I thank him, and am pleased by his attention.'

Another time the cat hid himself in a wheatfield, keeping the mouth of his bag wide open. Two partridges ventured in, and by pulling the cords tight he captured both of them. Off he went and presented them to the king, just as he had done with the rabbit from the warren. His Majesty was not less gratified by the brace of partridges, and handed the cat a present for himself.

For two or three months Puss went on in this way, every now and again taking to the king, as a present from his master, some game which he had caught. There came a day when he learned that the king intended to take his daughter, who was the most beautiful princess in the world, for an excursion along the river bank.

'If you will do as I tell you,' said Puss to his master, 'your fortune is made. You have only to go and bathe in the river at the spot which I shall point out to you. Leave the rest to me.'

The marquis of Carabas had no idea what plan was afoot, but did as the cat had directed.

While he was bathing the king drew near, and Puss at once began to cry out at the top of his voice:

'Help! help! the marquis of Carabas is drowning!'

At these shouts the king put his head out of the carriage window. He recognised the cat who had so often brought him game, and bade his escort go speedily to the help of the marquis of Carabas.

While they were pulling the poor marquis out of the river, Puss approached the carriage and explained to the king that while his master was bathing robbers had come and taken away his clothes, though he had cried 'Stop, thief!' at the top of his voice. As a matter of fact, the rascal had hidden them under a big stone. The king at once commanded the keepers of his wardrobe to go and select a suit of his finest clothes for the marquis of Carabas.

The king received the marquis with many compliments, and as the fine clothes which the latter had just put on set off his good looks (for he was handsome and comely in appearance), the king's daughter found him very much to her liking. Indeed, the marquis of Carabas had not bestowed more than two or three respectful but sentimental glances upon her when she fell madly in love with him. The king invited him to enter the coach and join the party.

Delighted to see his plan so successfully launched, the cat went on ahead, and presently came upon some peasants who were mowing a field.

'Listen, my good fellows,' said he; 'if you do not tell the king that the field which you are mowing belongs to the marquis of Carabas, you will all be chopped up into little pieces like mince-meat.'

In due course the king asked the mowers to whom the field on which they were at work belonged.

'It is the property of the marquis of Carabas,' they all cried with one voice, for the threat from Puss had frightened them.

'You have inherited a fine estate,' the king remarked to Carabas.

'As you see for yourself, Sire,' replied the marquis; 'this is a meadow which never fails to yield an abundant crop each year.'

Still travelling ahead, the cat came upon some harvesters.

'Listen, my good fellows,' said he; 'if you do not declare that every one of these fields belongs to the marquis of Carabas, you will all be chopped up into little bits like mince-meat.'

The king came by a moment later, and wished to know who was the owner of the fields in sight.

'It is the marquis of Carabas,' cried the harvesters.

At this the king was more pleased than ever with the marquis.

Preceding the coach on its journey, the cat made the same threat to all whom he met, and the king grew astonished at the great wealth of the marquis of Carabas.

Finally Master Puss reached a splendid castle, which belonged to an ogre. He was the richest ogre that had ever been known, for all the lands through which the king had passed were part of the castle domain.

The cat had taken care to find out who this ogre was, and what powers he possessed. He now asked for an interview, declaring that he was unwilling to pass so close to the castle without having the honour of paying his respects to the owner.

The ogre received him as civilly as an ogre can, and bade him sit down.

'I have been told,' said Puss, 'that you have the power to change yourself into any kind of animal – for example, that you can transform yourself into a lion or an elephant.'

'That is perfectly true,' said the ogre, curtly; 'and just to prove it you shall see me turn into a lion.'

Puss was so frightened on seeing a lion before him that he sprang on to the roof – not without difficulty and danger, for his boots were not meant for walking on the tiles.

Perceiving presently that the ogre had abandoned his transformation, Puss descended, and owned to having been thoroughly frightened.

'I have also been told,' he added, 'but I can scarcely believe it, that you have the further power to take the shape of the smallest animals – for example, that you can change yourself into a rat or a mouse. I confess that to me it seems quite impossible.'

'Impossible?' cried the ogre; 'you shall see!' And in the same moment he changed himself into a mouse, which began to run about the floor. No sooner did Puss see it than he pounced on it and ate it.

Presently the king came along, and noticing the ogre's beautiful mansion desired to visit it. The cat heard the rumble of the coach as it crossed the castle drawbridge, and running out to the courtyard cried to the king:

'Welcome, your Majesty, to the castle of the marquis of Carabas!'

'What's that?' cried the king. 'Is this castle also yours, marquis? Nothing could be finer than this courtyard and the buildings which I see all about. With your permission we will go inside and look round.'

The marquis gave his hand to the young princess, and followed the king as he led the way up the staircase. Entering a great hall they found there a magnificent collation. This had been prepared by the ogre for some friends who were to pay him a visit that very day. The latter had not dared to enter when they learned that the king was there.

The king was now quite as charmed with the excellent qualities of the marquis of Carabas as his daughter. The latter was completely captivated by him. Noting the great wealth of which the marquis was evidently possessed, and having quaffed several cups of wine, he turned to his host, saying:

'It rests with you, marquis, whether you will be my son-in-law.'

The marquis, bowing very low, accepted the honour which the king bestowed upon him. The very same day he married the princess.

Puss became a personage of great importance, and gave up hunting mice, except for amusement.

LITTLE TOM THUMB

Once upon a time there lived a wood-cutter and his wife, who had seven children, all boys. The eldest was only ten years old, and the youngest was seven. People were astonished that the wood-cutter had had so many children in so short a time, but the reason was that his wife delighted in children, and never had less than two at a time.

They were very poor, and their seven children were a great tax on them, for none of them was yet able to earn his own living. And they were troubled also because the youngest was very delicate and could not speak a word. They mistook for stupidity what was in reality a mark of good sense.

This youngest boy was very little. At his birth he was scarcely bigger than a man's thumb, and he was called in consequence 'Little Tom Thumb.' The poor child was the scapegoat of the family, and got the blame for everything. All the same, he was the sharpest and shrewdest of the brothers, and if he spoke but little he listened much.

There came a very bad year, when the famine was so great that these poor people resolved to get rid of their family. One evening, after the children had gone to bed, the wood-cutter was sitting in the chimney-corner with his wife. His heart was heavy with sorrow as he said to her:

'It must be plain enough to you that we can no longer feed our children. I cannot see them die of hunger before my eyes, and I have made up my mind to take them to-morrow to the forest and lose them there. It will be easy enough to manage, for while they are amusing themselves by collecting faggots we have only to disappear without their seeing us.'

'Ah!' cried the wood-cutter's wife, 'do you mean to say you are capable of letting your own children be lost?'

In vain did her husband remind her of their terrible poverty; she could not agree. She was poor, but she was their mother. In the end, however, reflecting what a grief it would be to see them die of hunger, she consented to the plan, and went weeping to bed.

Little Tom Thumb had heard all that was said. Having discovered, when in bed, that serious talk was going on, he had got up softly, and had slipped under his father's stool in order to listen without being seen. He went back to bed, but did not sleep a wink for the rest of the night, thinking over what he had better do. In the morning he rose very early and went to the edge of a brook. There he filled his pockets with little white pebbles and came quickly home again.

They all set out, and little Tom Thumb said not a word to his brothers of what he knew.

They went into a forest which was so dense that when only ten paces apart they could not see each other. The wood-cutter set about his work, and the children began to collect twigs to make faggots. Presently the father and mother, seeing them busy at their task, edged gradually away, and then hurried off in haste along a little narrow footpath.

When the children found they were alone they began to cry and call out with all their might. Little Tom Thumb let them cry, being confident that they would get back home again. For on the way he had dropped the little white stones which he carried in his pocket all along the path.

'Don't be afraid, brothers,' he said presently; 'our parents have left us here, but I will take you home again. Just follow me.'

They fell in behind him, and he led them straight to their house by the same path which they had taken to the forest. At first they dared not go in, but placed themselves against the door, where they could hear everything their father and mother were saying.

Now the wood-cutter and his wife had no sooner reached home than the lord of the manor sent them a sum of ten crowns which had been owing from him for a long time, and of which they had given up hope. This put new life into them, for the poor creatures were dying of hunger.

The wood-cutter sent his wife off to the butcher at once, and as it was such a long time since they had had anything to eat, she bought three times as much meat as a supper for two required.

When they found themselves once more at table, the wood-cutter's wife began to lament.

'Alas! where are our poor children now?' she said; 'they could make a good meal off what we have over. Mind you, William, it was you who wished to lose them: I declared over and over again that we should repent it. What are they doing now in that forest? Merciful heavens, perhaps the wolves have already eaten them! A monster you must be to lose your children in this way!'

At last the wood-cutter lost patience, for she repeated more than twenty times that he would repent it, and that she had told him so. He threatened to beat her if she did not hold her tongue.

It was not that the wood-cutter was less grieved than his wife, but she browbeat him, and he was of the same opinion as many other people, who like a woman to have the knack of saying the right thing, but not the trick of being always in the right.

'Alas!' cried the wood-cutter's wife, bursting into tears, 'where are now my children, my poor children?'

She said it once so loud that the children at the door heard it plainly. Together they all called out:

'Here we are! Here we are!'

She rushed to open the door for them, and exclaimed, as she embraced them:

'How glad I am to see you again, dear children! You must be very tired and very hungry. And you, Peterkin, how muddy you are – come and let me wash you!'

This Peterkin was her eldest son. She loved him more than all the others because he was inclined to be red-headed, and she herself was rather red.

They sat down at the table and ate with an appetite which it did their parents good to see. They all talked at once, as they recounted the fears they had felt in the forest.

The good souls were delighted to have their children with them again, and the pleasure continued as long as the ten crowns lasted. But when the money was all spent they relapsed into their former sadness. They again resolved to lose the children, and to lead them much further away than they had done the first time, so as to do the job thoroughly. But though they were careful not to speak openly about it, their conversation did not escape little Tom Thumb, who made up his mind to get out of the situation as he had done on the former occasion.

But though he got up early to go and collect his little stones, he found the door of the house doubly locked, and he could not carry out his plan.

He could not think what to do until the wood-cutter's wife gave them each a piece of bread for breakfast. Then it occurred to him to use the bread in place of the stones, by throwing crumbs along the path which they took, and he tucked it tight in his pocket.

Their parents led them into the thickest and darkest part

of the forest, and as soon as they were there slipped away by a side-path and left them. This did not much trouble little Tom Thumb, for he believed he could easily find the way back by means of the bread which he had scattered wherever he walked. But to his dismay he could not discover a single crumb. The birds had come along and eaten it all.

They were in sore trouble now, for with every step they strayed further, and became more and more entangled in the forest. Night came on and a terrific wind arose, which filled them with dreadful alarm. On every side they seemed to hear nothing but the howling of wolves which were coming to eat them up. They dared not speak or move.

In addition it began to rain so heavily that they were soaked to the skin. At every step they tripped and fell on the wet ground, getting up again covered with mud, not knowing what to do with their hands.

Little Tom Thumb climbed to the top of a tree, in an endeavour to see something. Looking all about him he espied, far away on the other side of the forest, a little light like that of a candle. He got down from the tree, and was terribly disappointed to find that when he was on the ground he could see nothing at all.

After they had walked some distance in the direction of the light, however, he caught a glimpse of it again as they were nearing the edge of the forest. At last they reached the house where the light was burning, but not without much anxiety, for every time they had to go down into a hollow they lost sight of it.

They knocked at the door, and a good dame opened to them. She asked them what they wanted.

Little Tom Thumb explained that they were poor children who had lost their way in the forest, and begged her, for pity's sake, to give them a night's lodging.

Noticing what bonny children they all were, the woman began to cry.

'Alas, my poor little dears!' she said; 'you do not know the place you have come to! Have you not heard that this is the house of an ogre who eats little children?'

'Alas, madam!' answered little Tom Thumb, trembling like all the rest of his brothers, 'what shall we do? One thing is very certain: if you do not take us in, the wolves of the forest will devour us this very night, and that being so we should prefer to be eaten by your husband. Perhaps he may take pity on us, if you will plead for us.'

The ogre's wife, thinking she might be able to hide them from her husband till the next morning, allowed them to come in, and put them to warm near a huge fire, where a whole sheep was cooking on the spit for the ogre's supper.

Just as they were beginning to get warm they heard two or three great bangs at the door. The ogre had returned. His wife hid them quickly under the bed and ran to open the door.

The first thing the ogre did was to ask whether supper was ready and the wine opened. Then without ado he sat down to table. Blood was still dripping from the sheep, but it seemed all the better to him for that. He sniffed to right and left, declaring that he could smell fresh flesh.

'Indeed!' said his wife. 'It must be the calf which I have just dressed that you smell.'

'*I smell fresh flesh,* I tell you!' shouted the ogre, eyeing his wife askance; 'and there is something going on here which I do not understand.'

With these words he got up from the table and went straight to the bed.

'Aha!' said he; 'so this is the way you deceive me, wicked woman that you are! I have a very great mind to eat you too! It's lucky for you that you are old and tough! I am expecting three ogre friends of mine to pay me a visit in the next few days, and here is a tasty dish which will just come in nicely for them!'

One after another he dragged the children out from under the bed.

The poor things threw themselves on their knees, imploring mercy; but they had to deal with the most cruel of all ogres. Far from pitying them, he was already devouring them with his eyes, and repeating to his wife that when cooked with a good sauce they would make most dainty morsels.

Off he went to get a large knife, which he sharpened, as he drew near the poor children, on a long stone in his left hand.

He had already seized one of them when his wife called out to him. 'What do you want to do it now for?' she said; 'will it not be time enough to-morrow?'

'Hold your tongue,' replied the ogre; 'they will be all the more tender.'

'But you have such a lot of meat,' rejoined his wife; 'look, there are a calf, two sheep, and half a pig.'

'You are right,' said the ogre; 'give them a good supper to fatten them up, and take them to bed.'

The good woman was overjoyed and brought them a splendid supper; but the poor little wretches were so cowed with fright that they could not eat.

As for the ogre, he went back to his drinking, very pleased to have such good entertainment for his friends. He drank a dozen cups more than usual, and was obliged to go off to bed early, for the wine had gone somewhat to his head.

Now the ogre had seven daughters who as yet were only children. These little ogresses all had the most lovely complexions, for, like their father, they ate fresh meat. But they had little round grey eyes, crooked noses, and very large mouths, with long and exceedingly sharp teeth, set far apart. They were not so very wicked at present, but they showed great promise, for already they were in the habit of killing little children to suck their blood.

They had gone to bed early, and were all seven in a great bed, each with a crown of gold upon her head.

In the same room there was another bed, equally large. Into this the ogre's wife put the seven little boys, and then went to sleep herself beside her husband.

Little Tom Thumb was fearful lest the ogre should suddenly regret that he had not cut the throats of himself and his brothers the evening before. Having noticed that the ogre's daughters all had golden crowns upon their heads, he got up in the middle of the night and softly placed his own cap and those of his brothers on their heads. Before doing so, he carefully removed the crowns of gold, putting them on his own and his brothers' heads. In this way, if the ogre were to feel like slaughtering them that night he would mistake the girls for the boys, and *vice versa*.

Things fell out just as he had anticipated. The ogre, waking up at midnight, regretted that he had postponed till the morrow what he could have done overnight. Jumping briskly out of bed, he seized his knife, crying: 'Now then, let's see how the little rascals are; we won't make the same mistake twice!'

He groped his way up to his daughters' room, and approached the bed in which were the seven little boys. All were sleeping, with the exception of little Tom Thumb, who was numb with fear when he felt the ogre's hand, as it touched the head of each brother in turn, reach his own.

'Upon my word,' said the ogre, as he felt the golden crowns; 'a nice job I was going to make of it! It is very evident that I drank a little too much last night!'

Forthwith he went to the bed where his daughters were, and here he felt the little boys' caps.

'Aha, here are the little scamps!' he cried; 'now for a smart bit of work!'

With these words, and without a moment's hesitation, he cut the throats of his seven daughters, and well satisfied with his work went back to bed beside his wife.

No sooner did little Tom Thumb hear him snoring than

he woke up his brothers, bidding them dress quickly and follow him. They crept quietly down to the garden, and jumped from the wall. All through the night they ran in haste and terror, without the least idea of where they were going.

When the ogre woke up he said to his wife:

'Go upstairs and dress those little rascals who were here last night.'

The ogre's wife was astonished at her husband's kindness, never doubting that he meant her to go and put on their clothes. She went upstairs, and was horrified to discover her seven daughters bathed in blood, with their throats cut.

She fell at once into a swoon, which is the way of most women in similar circumstances.

The ogre, thinking his wife was very long in carrying out his orders, went up to help her, and was no less astounded than his wife at the terrible spectacle which confronted him.

'What's this I have done?' he exclaimed. 'I will be revenged on the wretches, and quickly, too!'

He threw a jugful of water over his wife's face, and having brought her round ordered her to fetch his seven-league boots, so that he might overtake the children.

He set off over the countryside, and strode far and wide until he came to the road along which the poor children were travelling. They were not more than a few yards from their home when they saw the ogre striding from hill-top to hill-top, and stepping over rivers as though they were merely tiny streams.

Little Tom Thumb espied near at hand a cave in some rocks. In this he hid his brothers, and himself followed them in, while continuing to keep a watchful eye upon the movements of the ogre.

Now the ogre was feeling very tired after so much fruitless marching (for seven-league boots are very fatiguing to their wearer), and felt like taking a little rest. As it happened, he went and sat down on the very rock beneath which the little boys were hiding. Overcome with weariness, he had not sat there long before he fell asleep and began to snore so terribly that the poor children were as frightened as when he had held his great knife to their throats.

Little Tom Thumb was not so alarmed. He told his brothers to flee at once to their home while the ogre was still sleeping soundly, and not to worry about him. They took his advice and ran quickly home.

Little Tom Thumb now approached the ogre and gently pulled off his boots, which he at once donned himself. The boots were very heavy and very large, but being enchanted boots they had the faculty of growing larger or smaller according to the leg they had to suit. Consequently they always fitted as though they had been made for the wearer.

He went straight to the ogre's house, where he found the ogre's wife weeping over her murdered daughters.

'Your husband,' said little Tom Thumb, 'is in great danger, for he has been captured by a gang of thieves, and the latter have sworn to kill him if he does not hand over all his gold and silver. Just as they had the dagger at his throat, he caught sight of me and begged me to come to you and thus rescue him from his terrible plight. You are to give me everything of value which he possesses, without keeping back a thing, otherwise he will be slain without mercy. As the matter is urgent he wished me to wear his seven-league boots, to save time, and also to prove to you that I am no impostor.'

The ogre's wife, in great alarm, gave him immediately all that she had, for although this was an ogre who devoured little children, he was by no means a bad husband.

Little Tom Thumb, laden with all the ogre's wealth, forthwith repaired to his father's house, where he was received with great joy.

Many people do not agree about this last adventure, and pretend that little Tom Thumb never committed this theft from the ogre, and only took the seven-league boots, about which he had no compunction, since they were only used by the ogre for catching little children. These folks assert that they are in a position to know, having been guests at the wood-cutter's cottage. They further say that when little Tom Thumb had put on the ogre's boots, he went off to the Court, where he knew there was great anxiety concerning the result of a battle which was being fought by an army two hundred leagues away.

They say that he went to the king and undertook, if desired, to bring news of the army before the day was out; and that the king promised him a large sum of money if he could carry out his project.

Little Tom Thumb brought news that very night, and this first errand having brought him into notice, he made as much money as he wished. For not only did the king pay him handsomely to carry orders to the army, but many ladies at the court gave him anything he asked to get them news of their lovers, and this was his greatest source of income. He was occasionally entrusted by wives with letters to their husbands, but they paid him so badly, and this branch of the business brought him in so little, that he did not even bother to reckon what he made from it.

After acting as courier for some time, and amassing great wealth thereby, little Tom Thumb returned to his father's house, and was there greeted with the greatest joy imaginable. He made all his family comfortable, buying newly-created positions for his father and brothers. In this way he set them all up, not forgetting at the same time to look well after himself.

CLASSIC LITERATURE: WORDS AND PHRASES
adapted from the Collins English Dictionary

Accoucheur NOUN a male midwife or doctor ❏ *I think my sister must have had some general idea that I was a young offender whom an Accoucheur Policemen had taken up (on my birthday) and delivered over to her* (*Great Expectations* by Charles Dickens)

addled ADJ confused and unable to think properly ❏ *But she counted and counted till she got that addled* (*The Adventures of Huckleberry Finn* by Mark Twain)

admiration NOUN amazement or wonder ❏ *lifting up his hands and eyes by way of admiration* (*Gulliver's Travels* by Jonathan Swift)

afeard ADJ afeard means afraid ❏ *shake it–and don't be afeard* (*The Adventures of Huckleberry Finn* by Mark Twain)

affected VERB affected means to assume the appearance of ❏ *Hadst thou affected sweet divinity* (*Doctor Faustus 5.2* by Christopher Marlowe)

aground ADV when a boat runs aground, it touches the ground in a shallow part of the water and gets stuck ❏ *what kep' you?–boat get aground?* (*The Adventures of Huckleberry Finn* by Mark Twain)

ague NOUN a fever in which the patient has alternate hot and cold shivering fits ❏ *his exposure to the wet and cold had brought on fever and ague* (*Oliver Twist* by Charles Dickens)

alchemy ADJ false or worthless ❏ *all wealth alchemy* (*The Sun Rising* by John Donne)

all alike PHRASE the same all the time ❏ *Love, all alike* (*The Sun Rising* by John Donne)

alow and aloft PHRASE alow means in the lower part or bottom, and aloft means on the top, so alow and aloft means on the top and in the bottom or throughout ❏ *Someone's turned the chest out alow and aloft* (*Treasure Island* by Robert Louis Stevenson)

ambuscade NOUN ambuscade is not a proper word. Tom means an ambush, which is when a group of people attack their enemies, after hiding and waiting for them ❏ *and so we would lie in ambuscade, as he called it* (*The Adventures of Huckleberry Finn* by Mark Twain)

amiable ADJ likeable or pleasant ❏ *Such amiable qualities must speak for themselves* (*Pride and Prejudice* by Jane Austen)

amulet NOUN an amulet is a charm thought to drive away evil spirits. ❏ *uttered phrases at once occult and familiar, like the amulet worn on the heart* (*Silas Marner* by George Eliot)

amusement NOUN here amusement means a strange and disturbing puzzle ❏ *this was an amusement the other way* (*Robinson Crusoe* by Daniel Defoe)

ancient NOUN an ancient was the flag displayed on a ship to show which country it belongs to. It is also called the ensign ❏ *. her ancient and pendants out* (*Robinson Crusoe* by Daniel Defoe)

antic ADJ here antic means horrible or grotesque ❏ *armed and dressed after a very antic manner* (*Gulliver's Travels* by Jonathan Swift)

antics NOUN antics is an old word meaning clowns, or people who do silly things to make other people laugh ❏ *And point like antics at his triple crown* (*Doctor Faustus 3.2* by Christopher Marlowe)

appanage NOUN an appanage is a living allowance ❏ *As if loveliness were not the special prerogative of woman–her legitimate appanage and heritage!* (*Jane Eyre* by Charlotte Brontë)

appended VERB appended means attached or added to ❏ *and these words appended* (*Treasure Island* by Robert Louis Stevenson)

approver NOUN an approver is someone who gives evidence against someone he used to work with ❏ *Mr. Noah Claypole: receiving a free pardon from the Crown in consequence of being admitted approver against Fagin* (*Oliver Twist* by Charles Dickens)

areas NOUN the areas is the space, below street level, in front of the basement of a house ❏ *The Dodger had a vicious propensity, too, of pulling the caps from the heads of small boys and tossing them down areas* (*Oliver Twist* by Charles Dickens)

argument NOUN theme or important idea or subject which runs through a piece of writing ❏ *Thrice needful to the argument which now* (*The Prelude* by William Wordsworth)

artificially ADV artfully or cleverly ❏ *and he with a sharp flint sharpened very artificially* (*Gulliver's Travels* by Jonathan Swift)

artist NOUN here artist means a skilled workman ❏ *This man was a most ingenious artist* (*Gulliver's Travels* by Jonathan Swift)

assizes NOUN assizes were regular court sessions which a visiting judge was in charge of ❏ *you shall hang at the next assizes* (*Treasure Island* by Robert Louis Stevenson)

attraction NOUN gravitation, or Newton's theory of gravitation ❏ *he predicted the same fate to attraction* (*Gulliver's Travels* by Jonathan Swift)

aver VERB to aver is to claim something strongly ❏ *for Jem Rodney, the mole catcher, averred that one evening as he was returning homeward* (*Silas Marner* by George Eliot)

baby NOUN here baby means doll, which is a child's toy that looks like a small person ❏ *and skilful dressing her baby* (*Gulliver's Travels* by Jonathan Swift)

bagatelle NOUN bagatelle is a game rather like billiards and pool ❏ *Breakfast had been ordered at a pleasant little tavern, a mile or so away upon the rising ground beyond the green; and there was a bagatelle board in the room, in case we should desire to unbend our minds after the solemnity.* (*Great Expectations* by Charles Dickens)

bah EXCLAM Bah is an exclamation of frustration or anger ❏ *"Bah," said Scrooge.* (*A Christmas Carol* by Charles Dickens)

bairn NOUN a northern word for child ❏ *Who has taught you those fine words, my bairn?* (*Wuthering Heights* by Emily Brontë)

bait VERB to bait means to stop on a journey to take refreshment ❏ *So, when they stopped to bait the horse, and ate and drank and enjoyed themselves, I could touch nothing that they touched, but kept my fast unbroken.* (*David Copperfield* by Charles Dickens)

balustrade NOUN a balustrade is a row of vertical columns that form railings ❏ *but I mean to say you might have got a hearse up that staircase, and taken it broadwise, with the splinter-bar towards the wall, and the door towards the balustrades: and done it easy* (*A Christmas Carol* by Charles Dickens)

bandbox NOUN a large lightweight box for carrying bonnets or hats ❏ *I am glad I bought my bonnet, if it is only for the fun of having another bandbox* (*Pride and Prejudice* by Jane Austen)

barren NOUN a barren here is a stretch or expanse of barren land ❏ *a line of upright stones, continued the* *length of the barren* (*Wuthering Heights* by Emily Brontë)

basin NOUN a basin was a cup without a handle ❑ *who is drinking his tea out of a basin* (*Wuthering Heights* by Emily Brontë)

battalia NOUN the order of battle ❑ *till I saw part of his army in battalia* (*Gulliver's Travels* by Jonathan Swift)

battery NOUN a Battery is a fort or a place where guns are positioned ❑ *You bring the lot to me, at that old Battery over yonder* (*Great Expectations* by Charles Dickens)

battledore and shuttlecock NOUN The game battledore and shuttlecock was an early version of the game now known as badminton. The aim of the early game was simply to keep the shuttlecock from hitting the ground. ❑ *Battledore and shut-tlecock's a wery good game vhen you an't the shuttlecock and two lawyers the battledores, in which case it gets too excitin' to be pleasant* (*Pickwick Papers* by Charles Dickens)

beadle NOUN a beadle was a local official who had power over the poor ❑ *But these impertinences were speedily checked by the evidence of the surgeon, and the testimony of the beadle* (*Oliver Twist* by Charles Dickens)

bearings NOUN the bearings of a place are the measurements or directions that are used to find or locate it ❑ *the bearings of the island* (*Treasure Island* by Robert Louis Stevenson)

beaufet NOUN a beaufet was a sideboard ❑ *and sweet-cake from the beaufet* (*Emma* by Jane Austen)

beck NOUN a beck is a small stream ❑ *a beck which follows the bend of the glen* (*Wuthering Heights* by Emily Brontë)

bedight VERB decorated ❑ *and bedight with Christmas holly stuck into the top.* (*A Christmas Carol* by Charles Dickens)

Bedlam NOUN Bedlam was a lunatic asylum in London which had statues carved by Caius Gabriel Cibber at its entrance ❑ *Bedlam, and those carved maniacs at the gates* (*The Prelude* by William Wordsworth)

beeves NOUN oxen or castrated bulls which are animals used for pulling vehicles or carrying things ❑ *to deliver in every morning six beeves* (*Gulliver's Travels* by Jonathan Swift)

begot VERB created or caused ❑ *Begot in thee* (*On His Mistress* by John Donne)

behoof NOUN behoof means benefit ❑ *"Yes, young man," said he, releasing the handle of the article in question, retiring a step or two from my table, and speaking for the behoof of the landlord and waiter at the door* (*Great Expectations* by Charles Dickens)

berth NOUN a berth is a bed on a boat ❑ *this is the berth for me* (*Treasure Island* by Robert Louis Stevenson)

bevers NOUN a bever was a snack, or small portion of food, eaten between main meals ❑ *that buys me thirty meals a day and ten bevers* (*Doctor Faustus 2.1* by Christopher Marlowe)

bilge water NOUN the bilge is the widest part of a ship's bottom, and the bilge water is the dirty water that collects there ❑ *no gush of bilge-water had turned it to fetid puddle* (*Jane Eyre* by Charlotte Brontë)

bills NOUN bills is an old term meaning prescription. A prescription is the piece of paper on which your doctor writes an order for medicine and which you give to a chemist to get the medicine ❑ *Are not thy bills hung up as monuments* (*Doctor Faustus 1.1* by Christopher Marlowe)

black cap NOUN a judge wore a black cap when he was about to sentence a prisoner to death ❑ *The judge assumed the black cap, and the prisoner still stood with the same air and gesture.* (*Oliver Twist* by Charles Dickens)

boot-jack NOUN a wooden device to help take boots off ❑ *The speaker appeared to throw a boot-jack, or some such article, at the person he addressed* (*Oliver Twist* by Charles Dickens)

booty NOUN booty means treasure or prizes ❑ *would be inclined to give up their booty in payment of the dead man's debts* (*Treasure Island* by Robert Louis Stevenson)

Bow Street runner PHRASE Bow Street runners were the first British police force, set up by the author Henry Fielding in the eighteenth century ❑ *as would have convinced a judge or a Bow Street runner* (*Treasure Island* by Robert Louis Stevenson)

brawn NOUN brawn is a dish of meat which is set in jelly ❑ *Heaped up upon the floor, to form a kind of throne, were turkeys, geese, game, poultry, brawn, great joints of meat, suckling-pigs* (*A Christmas Carol* by Charles Dickens)

bray VERB when a donkey brays, it makes a loud, harsh sound ❑ *and she doesn't bray like a jackass* (*The Adventures of Huckleberry Finn* by Mark Twain)

break VERB in order to train a horse you first have to break it ❑ *"If a high-mettled creature like this," said he, "can't be broken by fair means, she will never be good for anything"* (*Black Beauty* by Anna Sewell)

bullyragging VERB bullyragging is an old word which means bullying. To bullyrag someone is to threaten or force someone to do something they don't want to do ❑ *and a lot of loafers bullyragging him for sport* (*The Adventures of Huckleberry Finn* by Mark Twain)

but PREP except for (this) ❑ *but this, all pleasures fancies be* (*The Good-Morrow* by John Donne)

by hand PHRASE by hand was a common expression of the time meaning that baby had been fed either using a spoon or a bottle rather than by breast-feeding ❑ *My sister, Mrs. Joe Gargery, was more than twenty years older than I, and had established a great reputation with herself . . . because she had bought me up "by hand"* (*Great Expectations* by Charles Dickens)

bye-spots NOUN bye-spots are lonely places ❑ *and bye-spots of tales rich with indigenous produce* (*The Prelude* by William Wordsworth)

calico NOUN calico is plain white fabric made from cotton ❑ *There was two old dirty calico dresses* (*The Adventures of Huckleberry Finn* by Mark Twain)

camp-fever NOUN camp-fever was another word for the disease typhus ❑ *during a severe camp-fever* (*Emma* by Jane Austen)

cant NOUN cant is insincere or empty talk ❑ *"Man," said the Ghost, "if man you be in heart, not adamant, forbear that wicked cant until you have discovered What the surplus is, and Where it is."* (*A Christmas Carol* by Charles Dickens)

canty ADJ canty means lively, full of life ❑ *My mother lived til eighty, a canty dame to the last* (*Wuthering Heights* by Emily Brontë)

canvas VERB to canvas is to discuss ❑ *We think so very differently on this point Mr Knightley, that there can be no use in canvassing it* (*Emma* by Jane Austen)

capital ADJ capital means excellent or extremely good ❑ *for it's capital, so shady, light, and big* (*Little Women* by Louisa May Alcott)

capstan NOUN a capstan is a device used on a ship to lift sails and anchors ❑ *capstans going, ships going out to sea, and unintelligible sea creatures roaring curses over the* *bulwarks at respondent lightermen* (*Great Expectations* by Charles Dickens)

case-bottle NOUN a square bottle designed to fit with others into a case ❏ *The spirit being set before him in a huge case-bottle, which had originally come out of some ship's locker* (*The Old Curiosity Shop* by Charles Dickens)

casement NOUN casement is a word meaning window. The teacher in *Nicholas Nickleby* misspells window showing what a bad teacher he is ❏ *W-i-n, win, d-e-r, der, winder, a casement.* (*Nicholas Nickleby* by Charles Dickens)

cataleptic ADJ a cataleptic fit is one in which the victim goes into a trancelike state and remains still for a long time ❏ *It was at this point in their history that Silas's cataleptic fit occurred during the prayer-meeting* (*Silas Marner* by George Eliot)

cauldron NOUN a cauldron is a large cooking pot made of metal ❏ *stirring a large cauldron which seemed to be full of soup* (*Alice's Adventures in Wonderland* by Lewis Carroll)

cephalic ADJ cephalic means to do with the head ❏ *with ink composed of a cephalic tincture* (*Gulliver's Travels* by Jonathan Swift)

chaise and four NOUN a closed four-wheel carriage pulled by four horses ❏ *he came down on Monday in a chaise and four to see the place* (*Pride and Prejudice* by Jane Austen)

chamberlain NOUN the main servant in a household ❏ *In those times a bed was always to be got there at any hour of the night, and the chamberlain, letting me in at his ready wicket, lighted the candle next in order on his shelf* (*Great Expectations* by Charles Dickens)

characters NOUN distinguishing marks ❏ *Impressed upon all forms the characters* (*The Prelude* by William Wordsworth)

chary ADJ cautious ❏ *I should have been chary of discussing my guardian too freely even with her* (*Great Expectations* by Charles Dickens)

cherishes VERB here cherishes means cheers or brightens ❏ *some philosophic song of Truth that cherishes our daily life* (*The Prelude* by William Wordsworth)

chickens' meat PHRASE chickens' meat is an old term which means chickens' feed or food ❏ *I had shook a bag of chickens' meat out in that place* (*Robinson Crusoe* by Daniel Defoe)

chimeras NOUN a chimera is an unrealistic idea or a wish which is unlikely to be fulfilled ❏ *with many other wild impossible chimeras* (*Gulliver's Travels* by Jonathan Swift)

chines NOUN chine is a cut of meat that includes part or all of the backbone of the animal ❏ *and they found hams and chines uncut* (*Silas Marner* by George Eliot)

chits NOUN chits is a slang word which means girls ❏ *I hate affected, niminy-piminy chits!* (*Little Women* by Louisa May Alcott)

chopped VERB chopped means come suddenly or accidentally ❏ *if I had chopped upon them* (*Robinson Crusoe* by Daniel Defoe)

chute NOUN a narrow channel ❏ *One morning about day-break, I found a canoe and crossed over a chute to the main shore* (*The Adventures of Huckleberry Finn* by Mark Twain)

circumspection NOUN careful observation of events and circumstances; caution ❏ *I honour your circumspection* (*Pride and Prejudice* by Jane Austen)

clambered VERB clambered means to climb somewhere with difficulty, usually using your hands and your feet ❏ *he clambered up and down stairs* (*Treasure Island* by Robert Louis Stevenson)

clime NOUN climate ❏ *no season knows nor clime* (*The Sun Rising* by John Donne)

clinched VERB clenched ❏ *the tops whereof I could but just reach with my fist clinched* (*Gulliver's Travels* by Jonathan Swift)

close chair NOUN a close chair is a sedan chair, which is an covered chair which has room for one person. The sedan chair is carried on two poles by two men, one in front and one behind ❏ *persuaded even the Empress herself to let me hold her in her close chair* (*Gulliver's Travels* by Jonathan Swift)

clown NOUN clown here means peasant or person who lives off the land ❏ *In ancient days by emperor and clown* (*Ode on a Nightingale* by John Keats)

coalheaver NOUN a coalheaver loaded coal onto ships using a spade ❏ *Good, strong, wholesome medicine, as was given with great success to two Irish labourers and a coalheaver* (*Oliver Twist* by Charles Dickens)

coal-whippers NOUN men who worked at docks using machines to load coal onto ships ❏ *here, were colliers by the score and score, with the coal-whippers plunging off stages on deck* (*Great Expectations* by Charles Dickens)

cobweb NOUN a cobweb is the net which a spider makes for catching insects ❏ *the walls and ceilings were all hung round with cobwebs* (*Gulliver's Travels* by Jonathan Swift)

coddling VERB coddling means to treat someone too kindly or protect them too much ❏ *and I've been coddling the fellow as if I'd been his grandmother* (*Little Women* by Louisa May Alcott)

coil NOUN coil means noise or fuss or disturbance ❏ *What a coil is there?* (*Doctor Faustus 4.7* by Christopher Marlowe)

collared VERB to collar something is a slang term which means to capture.

In this sentence, it means he stole it [the money] ❏ *he collared it* (*The Adventures of Huckleberry Finn* by Mark Twain)

colling VERB colling is an old word which means to embrace and kiss ❏ *and no clasping and colling at all* (*Tess of the D'Urbervilles* by Thomas Hardy)

colloquies NOUN colloquy is a formal conversation or dialogue ❏ *Such colloquies have occupied many a pair of pale-faced weavers* (*Silas Marner* by George Eliot)

comfit NOUN sugar-covered pieces of fruit or nut eaten as sweets ❏ *and pulled out a box of comfits* (*Alice's Adventures in Wonderland* by Lewis Carroll)

coming out VERB when a girl came out in society it meant she was of marriageable age. In order to "come out" girls were expecting to attend balls and other parties during a season ❏ *The younger girls formed hopes of coming out a year or two sooner than they might otherwise have done* (*Pride and Prejudice* by Jane Austen)

commit VERB commit means arrest or stop ❏ *Commit the rascals* (*Doctor Faustus 4.7* by Christopher Marlowe)

commodious ADJ commodious means convenient ❏ *the most commodious and effectual ways* (*Gulliver's Travels* by Jonathan Swift)

commons NOUN commons is an old term meaning food shared with others ❏ *his pauper assistants ranged themselves behind him; the gruel was served out; and a long grace was said over the short commons.* (*Oliver Twist* by Charles Dickens)

complacency NOUN here complacency means a desire to please others. To-day complacency means feeling pleased with oneself without good reason. ❏ *Twas thy power that raised the first complacency in me* (*The Prelude* by William Wordsworth)

complaisance NOUN complaisance was eagerness to please ❑ *we cannot wonder at his complaisance* (*Pride and Prejudice* by Jane Austen)

complaisant ADJ complaisant means polite ❑ *extremely cheerful and complaisant to their guest* (*Gulliver's Travels* by Jonathan Swift)

conning VERB conning means learning by heart ❑ *Or conning more* (*The Prelude* by William Wordsworth)

consequent NOUN consequence ❑ *as avarice is the necessary consequent of old age* (*Gulliver's Travels* by Jonathan Swift)

consorts NOUN concerts ❑ *The King, who delighted in music, had frequent consorts at Court* (*Gulliver's Travels* by Jonathan Swift)

conversible ADJ conversible meant easy to talk to, companionable ❑ *He can be a conversible companion* (*Pride and Prejudice* by Jane Austen)

copper NOUN a copper is a large pot that can be heated directly over a fire ❑ *He gazed in stupefied astonishment on the small rebel for some seconds, and then clung for support to the copper* (*Oliver Twist* by Charles Dickens)

copper-stick NOUN a copper-stick is the long piece of wood used to stir washing in the copper (or boiler) which was usually the biggest cooking pot in the house ❑ *It was Christmas Eve, and I had to stir the pudding for next day, with a copper-stick, from seven to eight by the Dutch clock* (*Great Expectations* by Charles Dickens)

counting-house NOUN a counting-house is a place where accountants work ❑ *Once upon a time–of all the good days in the year, on Christmas Eve–old Scrooge sat busy in his counting-house* (*A Christmas Carol* by Charles Dickens)

courtier NOUN a courtier is someone who attends the king or queen–a member of the court ❑ *next the ten courtiers;* (*Alice's Adventures in Wonderland* by Lewis Carroll)

covies NOUN covies were flocks of partridges ❑ *and will save all of the best covies for you* (*Pride and Prejudice* by Jane Austen)

cowed VERB cowed means frightened or intimidated ❑ *it cowed me more than the pain* (*Treasure Island* by Robert Louis Stevenson)

cozened VERB cozened means tricked or deceived ❑ *Do you remember, sir, how you cozened me* (*Doctor Faustus 4.7* by Christopher Marlowe)

cravats NOUN a cravat is a folded cloth that a man wears wrapped around his neck as a decorative item of clothing ❑ *we'd 'a' slept in our cravats to-night* (*The Adventures of Huckleberry Finn* by Mark Twain)

crock and dirt PHRASE crock and dirt is an old expression meaning soot and dirt ❑ *and the mare catching cold at the door, and the boy grimed with crock and dirt* (*Great Expectations* by Charles Dickens)

crockery NOUN here crockery means pottery ❑ *By one of the parrots was a cat made of crockery* (*The Adventures of Huckleberry Finn* by Mark Twain)

crooked sixpence PHRASE it was considered unlucky to have a bent sixpence ❑ *You've got the beauty, you see, and I've got the luck, so you must keep me by you for your crooked sixpence* (*Silas Marner* by George Eliot)

croquet NOUN croquet is a traditional English summer game in which players try to hit wooden balls through hoops ❑ *and once she remembered trying to box her own ears for having cheated herself in a game of croquet* (*Alice's Adventures in Wonderland* by Lewis Carroll)

cross PREP across ❑ *The two great streets, which run cross and divide it into four quarters* (*Gulliver's Travels* by Jonathan Swift)

culpable ADJ if you are culpable for something it means you are to blame ❑ *deep are the sorrows that spring from false ideas for which no man is culpable.* (*Silas Marner* by George Eliot)

cultured ADJ cultivated ❑ *Nor less when spring had warmed the cultured Vale* (*The Prelude* by William Wordsworth)

cupidity NOUN cupidity is greed ❑ *These people hated me with the hatred of cupidity and disappointment.* (*Great Expectations* by Charles Dickens)

curricle NOUN an open two-wheeled carriage with one seat for the driver and space for a single passenger ❑ *and they saw a lady and a gentleman in a curricle* (*Pride and Prejudice* by Jane Austen)

cynosure NOUN a cynosure is something that strongly attracts attention or admiration ❑ *Then I thought of Eliza and Georgiana; I beheld one the cynosure of a ballroom, the other the inmate of a convent cell* (*Jane Eyre* by Charlotte Brontë)

dalliance NOUN someone's dalliance with something is a brief involvement with it ❑ *nor sporting in the dalliance of love* (*Doctor Faustus Chorus* by Christopher Marlowe)

darkling ADV darkling is an archaic way of saying in the dark ❑ *Darkling I listen* (*Ode on a Nightingale* by John Keats)

delf-case NOUN a sideboard for holding dishes and crockery ❑ *at the pewter dishes and delf-case* (*Wuthering Heights* by Emily Brontë)

determined ■ VERB here determined means ended ❑ *and be out of vogue when that was determined* (*Gulliver's Travels* by Jonathan Swift) ■ VERB determined can mean to have been learned or found especially by investigation or experience ❑ *All the sensitive feelings it wounded so cruelly, all the shame and misery it kept alive within my breast, became more poignant as I thought of this; and I determined that the life was unendurable* (*David Copperfield* by Charles Dickens)

Deuce NOUN a slang term for the Devil ❑ *Ah, I dare say I did. Deuce take me, he added suddenly, I know I did. I find I am not quite unscrewed yet.* (*Great Expectations* by Charles Dickens)

diabolical ADJ diabolical means devilish or evil ❑ *and with a thousand diabolical expressions* (*Treasure Island* by Robert Louis Stevenson)

direction NOUN here direction means address ❑ *Elizabeth was not surprised at it, as Jane had written the direction remarkably ill* (*Pride and Prejudice* by Jane Austen)

discover VERB to make known or announce ❑ *the Emperor would discover the secret while I was out of his power* (*Gulliver's Travels* by Jonathan Swift)

dissemble VERB hide or conceal ❑ *Dissemble nothing* (*On His Mistress* by John Donne)

dissolve VERB dissolve here means to release from life, to die ❑ *Fade far away, dissolve, and quite forget* (*Ode on a Nightingale* by John Keats)

distrain VERB to distrain is to seize the property of someone who is in debt in compensation for the money owed ❑ *for he's threatening to distrain for it* (*Silas Marner* by George Eliot)

Divan NOUN a Divan was originally a Turkish council of state–the name was transferred to the couches they sat on and is used to mean this in English ❑ *Mr Brass applauded this picture very much, and the bed being soft and comfortable, Mr Quilp determined to use it, both as a sleeping place by night and as a kind of Divan by day.* (*The Old Curiosity Shop* by Charles Dickens)

divorcement NOUN separation ❑ *By all pains which want and divorcement* *hath* (*On His Mistress* by John Donne)

dog in the manger, PHRASE this phrase describes someone who prevents you from enjoying something that they themselves have no need for ❑ *You are a dog in the manger, Cathy, and desire no one to be loved but yourself* (*Wuthering Heights* by Emily Brontë)

dolorifuge NOUN dolorifuge is a word which Thomas Hardy invented. It means pain-killer or comfort ❑ *as a species of dolorifuge* (*Tess of the D'Urbervilles* by Thomas Hardy)

dome NOUN building ❑ *that river and that mouldering dome* (*The Prelude* by William Wordsworth)

domestic NOUN here domestic means a person's management of the house ❑ *to give some account of my domestic* (*Gulliver's Travels* by Jonathan Swift)

dunce NOUN a dunce is another word for idiot ❑ *Do you take me for a dunce? Go on?* (*Alice's Adventures in Wonderland* by Lewis Carroll)

Ecod EXCLAM a slang exclamation meaning "oh God!" ❑ *"Ecod," replied Wemmick, shaking his head, "that's not my trade."* (*Great Expectations* by Charles Dickens)

egg-hot NOUN an egg-hot (see also "flip" and "negus") was a hot drink made from beer and eggs, sweetened with nutmeg ❑ *She fainted when she saw me return, and made a little jug of egg-hot afterwards to console us while we talked it over.* (*David Copperfield* by Charles Dickens)

encores NOUN an encore is a short extra performance at the end of a longer one, which the entertainer gives because the audience has enthusiastically asked for it ❑ *we want a little something to answer encores with, anyway* (*The Adventures of Huckleberry Finn* by Mark Twain)

equipage NOUN an elegant and impressive carriage ❑ *and besides, the equipage did not answer to any of*

their neighbours (*Pride and Prejudice* by Jane Austen)

exordium NOUN an exordium is the opening part of a speech ❑ *"Now, Handel," as if it were the grave beginning of a portentous business exordium, he had suddenly given up that tone* (*Great Expectations* by Charles Dickens)

expect VERB here expect means to wait for ❑ *to expect his farther commands* (*Gulliver's Travels* by Jonathan Swift)

familiars NOUN familiars means spirits or devils who come to someone when they are called ❑ *I'll turn all the lice about thee into familiars* (*Doctor Faustus* 1.4 by Christopher Marlowe)

fantods NOUN a fantod is a person who fidgets or can't stop moving nervously ❑ *It most give me the fantods* (*The Adventures of Huckleberry Finn* by Mark Twain)

farthing NOUN a farthing is an old unit of British currency which was worth a quarter of a penny ❑ *Not a farthing less. A great many back-payments are included in it, I assure you.* (*A Christmas Carol* by Charles Dickens)

farthingale NOUN a hoop worn under a skirt to extend it ❑ *A bell with an old voice–which I dare say in its time had often said to the house, Here is the green farthingale* (*Great Expectations* by Charles Dickens)

favours NOUN here favours is an old word which means ribbons ❑ *A group of humble mourners entered the gate: wearing white favours* (*Oliver Twist* by Charles Dickens)

feigned VERB pretend or pretending ❑ *not my feigned page* (*On His Mistress* by John Donne)

fence ■ NOUN a fence is someone who receives and sells stolen goods ❑ *What are you up to? Ill-treating the boys, you covetous, avaricious, in-sa-ti-a-ble old fence?* (*Oliver Twist* by

Charles Dickens) ■ NOUN defence or protection ❏ *but honesty hath no fence against superior cunning* (*Gulliver's Travels* by Jonathan Swift)

fess ADJ fess is an old word which means pleased or proud ❏ *You'll be fess enough, my poppet* (*Tess of the D'Urbervilles* by Thomas Hardy)

fettered ADJ fettered means bound in chains or chained ❏ *"You are fettered," said Scrooge, trembling. "Tell me why?"* (*A Christmas Carol* by Charles Dickens)

fidges VERB fidges means fidgets, which is to keep moving your hands slightly because you are nervous or excited ❏ *Look, Jim, how my fingers fidges* (*Treasure Island* by Robert Louis Stevenson)

finger-post NOUN a finger-post is a sign-post showing the direction to different places ❏ *"The gallows," continued Fagin, "the gallows, my dear, is an ugly finger-post, which points out a very short and sharp turning that has stopped many a bold fellow's career on the broad highway."* (*Oliver Twist* by Charles Dickens)

fire-irons NOUN fire-irons are tools kept by the side of the fire to either cook with or look after the fire ❏ *the fire-irons came first* (*Alice's Adventures in Wonderland* by Lewis Carroll)

fire-plug NOUN a fire-plug is another word for a fire hydrant ❏ *The pony looked with great attention into a fire-plug, which was near him, and appeared to be quite absorbed in contemplating it* (*The Old Curiosity Shop* by Charles Dickens)

flank NOUN flank is the side of an animal ❏ *And all her silken flanks with garlands dressed* (*Ode on a Grecian Urn* by John Keats)

flip NOUN a flip is a drink made from warmed ale, sugar, spice and beaten egg ❏ *The events of the day, in combination with the twins, if not with the flip, had made Mrs.*

Micawber hysterical, and she shed tears as she replied (*David Copperfield* by Charles Dickens)

flit VERB flit means to move quickly ❏ *and if he had meant to flit to Thrushcross Grange* (*Wuthering Heights* by Emily Brontë)

floorcloth NOUN a floorcloth was a hard-wearing piece of canvas used instead of carpet ❏ *This avenging phantom was ordered to be on duty at eight on Tuesday morning in the hall (it was two feet square, as charged for floorcloth)* (*Great Expectations* by Charles Dickens)

fly-driver NOUN a fly-driver is a carriage drawn by a single horse ❏ *The fly-drivers, among whom I inquired next, were equally jocose and equally disrespectful* (*David Copperfield* by Charles Dickens)

fob NOUN a small pocket in which a watch is kept ❏ *"Certain," replied the man, drawing a gold watch from his fob* (*Oliver Twist* by Charles Dickens)

folly NOUN folly means foolishness or stupidity ❏ *the folly of beginning a work* (*Robinson Crusoe* by Daniel Defoe)

fond ADJ fond means foolish ❏ *Fond worldling* (*Doctor Faustus 5.2* by Christopher Marlowe)

fondness NOUN silly or foolish affection ❏ *They have no fondness for their colts or foals* (*Gulliver's Travels* by Jonathan Swift)

for his fancy PHRASE for his fancy means for his liking or as he wanted ❏ *and as I did not obey quick enough for his fancy* (*Treasure Island* by Robert Louis Stevenson)

forlorn ADJ lost or very upset ❏ *you are from that day forlorn* (*Gulliver's Travels* by Jonathan Swift)

foster-sister NOUN a foster-sister was someone brought up by the same nurse or in the same household ❏ *I had been his foster-sister* (*Wuthering Heights* by Emily Brontë)

fox-fire NOUN fox-fire is a weak glow that is given off by decaying, rotten wood ❑ *what we must have was a lot of them rotten chunks that's called fox-fire* (*The Adventures of Huckleberry Finn* by Mark Twain)

frozen sea PHRASE the Arctic Ocean ❑ *into the frozen sea* (*Gulliver's Travels* by Jonathan Swift)

gainsay VERB to gainsay something is to say it isn't true or to deny it ❑ *"So she had," cried Scrooge. "You're right. I'll not gainsay it, Spirit. God forbid!"* (*A Christmas Carol* by Charles Dickens)

gaiters NOUN gaiters were leggings made of a cloth or piece of leather which covered the leg from the knee to the ankle ❑ *Mr Knightley was hard at work upon the lower buttons of his thick leather gaiters* (*Emma* by Jane Austen)

galluses NOUN galluses is an old spelling of gallows, and here means suspenders. Suspenders are straps worn over someone's shoulders and fastened to their trousers to prevent the trousers falling down ❑ *and home-knit galluses* (*The Adventures of Huckleberry Finn* by Mark Twain)

galoot NOUN a sailor but also a clumsy person ❑ *and maybe a galoot on it chopping* (*The Adventures of Huckleberry Finn* by Mark Twain)

gayest ADJ gayest means the most lively and bright or merry ❑ *Beth played her gayest march* (*Little Women* by Louisa May Alcott)

gem NOUN here gem means jewellery ❑ *the mountain shook off turf and flower, had only heath for raiment and crag for gem* (*Jane Eyre* by Charlotte Brontë)

giddy ADJ giddy means dizzy ❑ *and I wish you wouldn't keep appearing and vanishing so suddenly; you make one quite giddy.* (*Alice's Adventures in Wonderland* by Lewis Carroll)

gig NOUN a light two-wheeled carriage ❑ *when a gig drove up to the garden gate: out of which there jumped a fat gentleman* (*Oliver Twist* by Charles Dickens)

gladsome ADJ gladsome is an old word meaning glad or happy ❑ *Nobody ever stopped him in the street to say, with gladsome looks* (*A Christmas Carol* by Charles Dickens)

glen NOUN a glen is a small valley; the word is used commonly in Scotland ❑ *a beck which follows the bend of the glen* (*Wuthering Heights* by Emily Brontë)

gravelled VERB gravelled is an old term which means to baffle or defeat someone ❑ *Gravelled the pastors of the German Church* (*Doctor Faustus 1.1* by Christopher Marlowe)

grinder NOUN a grinder was a private tutor ❑ *but that when he had had the happiness of marrying Mrs Pocket very early in his life, he had impaired his prospects and taken up the calling of a Grinder* (*Great Expectations* by Charles Dickens)

gruel NOUN gruel is a thin, watery cornmeal or oatmeal soup ❑ *and the little saucepan of gruel (Scrooge had a cold in his head) upon the hob.* (*A Christmas Carol* by Charles Dickens)

guinea, half a NOUN half a guinea was ten shillings and sixpence ❑ *but lay out half a guinea at Ford's* (*Emma* by Jane Austen)

gull VERB gull is an old term which means to fool or deceive someone ❑ *Hush, I'll gull him supernaturally* (*Doctor Faustus 3.4* by Christopher Marlowe)

gunnel NOUN the gunnel, or gunwale, is the upper edge of a boat's side ❑ *But he put his foot on the gunnel and rocked her* (*The Adventures of Huckleberry Finn* by Mark Twain)

gunwale NOUN the side of a ship ❑ *He dipped his hand in the water over the boat's gunwale* (*Great Expectations* by Charles Dickens)

Gytrash NOUN a Gytrash is an omen of misfortune to the superstitious, usually taking the form of a hound ❑ *I remembered certain of Bessie's tales, wherein figured a North-of-England spirit, called a "Gytrash"* (*Jane Eyre* by Charlotte Brontë)

hackney-cabriolet NOUN a two-wheeled carriage with four seats for hire and pulled by a horse ❑ *A hackney-cabriolet was in waiting; with the same vehemence which she had exhibited in addressing Oliver, the girl pulled him in with her, and drew the curtains close.* (*Oliver Twist* by Charles Dickens)

hackney-coach NOUN a four-wheeled horse-drawn vehicle for hire ❑ *The twilight was beginning to close in, when Mr. Brownlow alighted from a hackney-coach at his own door, and knocked softly.* (*Oliver Twist* by Charles Dickens)

haggler NOUN a haggler is someone who travels from place to place selling small goods and items ❑ *when I be plain Jack Durbeyfield, the haggler* (*Tess of the D'Urbervilles* by Thomas Hardy)

halter NOUN a halter is a rope or strap used to lead an animal or to tie it up ❑ *I had of course long been used to a halter and a headstall* (*Black Beauty* by Anna Sewell)

hamlet NOUN a hamlet is a small village or a group of houses in the countryside ❑ *down from the hamlet* (*Treasure Island* by Robert Louis Stevenson)

hand-barrow NOUN a hand-barrow is a device for carrying heavy objects. It is like a wheelbarrow except that it has handles, rather than wheels, for moving the barrow ❑ *his sea chest following behind him in a hand-barrow* (*Treasure Island* by Robert Louis Stevenson)

handspike NOUN a handspike was a stick which was used as a lever ❑ *a bit of stick like a handspike* (*Treasure Island* by Robert Louis Stevenson)

haply ADV haply means by chance or perhaps ❑ *And haply the Queen-Moon is on her throne* (*Ode on a Nightingale* by John Keats)

harem NOUN the harem was the part of the house where the women lived ❑ *mostly they hang round the harem* (*The Adventures of Huckleberry Finn* by Mark Twain)

hautboys NOUN hautboys are oboes ❑ *sausages and puddings resembling flutes and hautboys* (*Gulliver's Travels* by Jonathan Swift)

hawker NOUN a hawker is someone who sells goods to people as he travels rather than from a fixed place like a shop ❑ *to buy some stockings from a hawker* (*Treasure Island* by Robert Louis Stevenson)

hawser NOUN a hawser is a rope used to tie up or tow a ship or boat ❑ *Again among the tiers of shipping, in and out, avoiding rusty chain-cables, frayed hempen hawsers* (*Great Expectations* by Charles Dickens)

headstall NOUN the headstall is the part of the bridle or halter that goes around a horse's head ❑ *I had of course long been used to a halter and a headstall* (*Black Beauty* by Anna Sewell)

hearken VERB hearken means to listen ❑ *though we sometimes stopped to lay hold of each other and hearken* (*Treasure Island* by Robert Louis Stevenson)

heartless ADJ here heartless means without heart or dejected ❑ *I am not heartless* (*The Prelude* by William Wordsworth)

hebdomadal ADJ hebdomadal means weekly ❑ *It was the hebdomadal treat to which we all looked forward from Sabbath to Sabbath* (*Jane Eyre* by Charlotte Brontë)

highwaymen NOUN highwaymen were people who stopped travellers and robbed them ❑ *We are highwaymen* (*The Adventures of Huckleberry Finn* by Mark Twain)

hinds NOUN hinds means farm hands, or people who work on a farm ❑ *He called his hinds about him* (*Gulliver's Travels* by Jonathan Swift)

histrionic ADJ if you refer to someone's behaviour as histrionic, you are being critical of it because it is dramatic and exaggerated ❑ *But the histrionic muse is the darling* (*The Adventures of Huckleberry Finn* by Mark Twain)

hogs NOUN hogs is another word for pigs ❑ *Tom called the hogs "ingots"* (*The Adventures of Huckleberry Finn* by Mark Twain)

horrors NOUN the horrors are a fit, called delirium tremens, which is caused by drinking too much alcohol ❑ *I'll have the horrors* (*Treasure Island* by Robert Louis Stevenson)

huffy ADJ huffy means to be obviously annoyed or offended about something ❑ *They will feel that more than angry speeches or huffy actions* (*Little Women* by Louisa May Alcott)

hulks NOUN hulks were prison-ships ❑ *The miserable companion of thieves and ruffians, the fallen outcast of low haunts, the associate of the scourings of the jails and hulks* (*Oliver Twist* by Charles Dickens)

humbug NOUN humbug means nonsense or rubbish ❑ *"Bah," said Scrooge. "Humbug!"* (*A Christmas Carol* by Charles Dickens)

humours NOUN it was believed that there were four fluids in the body called humours which decided the temperament of a person depending on how much of each fluid was present ❑ *other peccant humours* (*Gulliver's Travels* by Jonathan Swift)

husbandry NOUN husbandry is farming animals ❑ *bad husbandry were plentifully anointing their wheels* (*Silas Marner* by George Eliot)

huswife NOUN a huswife was a small sewing kit ❑ *but I had put my huswife on it* (*Emma* by Jane Austen)

ideal ADJ ideal in this context means imaginary ❑ *I discovered the yell was not ideal* (*Wuthering Heights* by Emily Brontë)

If our two PHRASE if both our ❑ *If our two loves be one* (*The Good-Morrow* by John Donne)

ignis-fatuus NOUN ignis-fatuus is the light given out by burning marsh gases, which lead careless travellers into danger ❑ *it is madness in all women to let a secret love kindle within them, which, if unreturned and unknown, must devour the life that feeds it; and, if discovered and responded to, must lead ignis-fatuus-like, into miry wilds whence there is no extrication.* (*Jane Eyre* by Charlotte Brontë)

imaginations NOUN here imaginations means schemes or plans ❑ *soon drove out those imaginations* (*Gulliver's Travels* by Jonathan Swift)

impressible ADJ impressible means open or impressionable ❑ *for Marner had one of those impressible, self-doubting natures* (*Silas Marner* by George Eliot)

in good intelligence PHRASE friendly with each other ❑ *that these two persons were in good intelligence with each other* (*Gulliver's Travels* by Jonathan Swift)

inanity NOUN inanity is silliness or dull stupidity ❑ *Do we not wile away moments of inanity* (*Silas Marner* by George Eliot)

incivility NOUN incivility means rudeness or impoliteness ❑ *if it's only for a piece of incivility like to-night's* (*Treasure Island* by Robert Louis Stevenson)

indigenae NOUN indigenae means natives or people from that area ❑ *an exotic that the surly indigenae will not recognise for kin* (*Wuthering Heights* by Emily Brontë)

indocible ADJ unteachable ❑ *so they were the most restive and indocible* (*Gulliver's Travels* by Jonathan Swift)

ingenuity NOUN inventiveness ❏ *entreated me to give him something as an encouragement to ingenuity* (*Gulliver's Travels* by Jonathan Swift)

ingots NOUN an ingot is a lump of a valuable metal like gold, usually shaped like a brick ❏ *Tom called the hogs "ingots"* (*The Adventures of Huckleberry Finn* by Mark Twain)

inkstand NOUN an inkstand is a pot which was put on a desk to contain either ink or pencils and pens ❏ *throwing an inkstand at the Lizard as she spoke* (*Alice's Adventures in Wonderland* by Lewis Carroll)

inordinate ADJ without order. To-day inordinate means "excessive". ❏ *Though yet untutored and inordinate* (*The Prelude* by William Wordsworth)

intellectuals NOUN here intellectuals means the minds (of the workmen) ❏ *those instructions they give being too refined for the intellectuals of their workmen* (*Gulliver's Travels* by Jonathan Swift)

interview NOUN meeting ❏ *By our first strange and fatal interview* (*On His Mistress* by John Donne)

jacks NOUN jacks are rods for turning a spit over a fire ❏ *It was a small bit of pork suspended from the kettle hanger by a string passed through a large door key, in a way known to primitive housekeepers unpossessed of jacks* (*Silas Marner* by George Eliot)

jews-harp NOUN a jews-harp is a small, metal, musical instrument that is played by the mouth ❏ *A jews-harp's plenty good enough for a rat* (*The Adventures of Huckleberry Finn* by Mark Twain)

jorum NOUN a large bowl ❏ *while Miss Skiffins brewed such a jorum of tea, that the pig in the back premises became strongly excited* (*Great Expectations* by Charles Dickens)

jostled VERB jostled means bumped or pushed by someone or some people

being jostled himself into the kennel (*Gulliver's Travels* by Jonathan Swift)

keepsake NOUN a keepsake is a gift which reminds someone of an event or of the person who gave it to them. ❏ *books and ornaments they had in their boudoirs at home: keepsakes that different relations had presented to them* (*Jane Eyre* by Charlotte Brontë)

kenned VERB kenned means knew ❏ *though little kenned the lamplighter that he had any company but Christmas!* (*A Christmas Carol* by Charles Dickens)

kennel NOUN kennel means gutter, which is the edge of a road next to the pavement, where rain water collects and flows away ❏ *being jostled himself into the kennel* (*Gulliver's Travels* by Jonathan Swift)

knock-knee ADJ knock-knee means slanted, at an angle. ❏ *LOT 1 was marked in whitewashed knock-knee letters on the brewhouse* (*Great Expectations* by Charles Dickens)

ladylike ADJ to be ladylike is to behave in a polite, dignified and graceful way ❏ *No, winking isn't ladylike* (*Little Women* by Louisa May Alcott)

lapse NOUN flow ❏ *Stealing with silent lapse to join the brook* (*The Prelude* by William Wordsworth)

larry NOUN larry is an old word which means commotion or noisy celebration ❏ *That was all a part of the larry!* (*Tess of the D'Urbervilles* by Thomas Hardy)

laths NOUN laths are strips of wood ❏ *The panels shrunk, the windows cracked; fragments of plaster fell out of the ceiling, and the naked laths were shown instead* (*A Christmas Carol* by Charles Dickens)

leer NOUN a leer is an unpleasant smile ❏ *with a kind of leer* (*Treasure Island* by Robert Louis Stevenson)

lenitives NOUN these are different kinds of drugs or medicines: lenitives and palliatives were pain relievers; aperitives were laxatives; abstersives caused vomiting; corrosives destroyed human tissue; restringents caused constipation; cephalalgics stopped headaches; icterics were used as medicine for jaundice; apophlegmatics were cough medicine, and acoustics were cures for the loss of hearing ❑ *lenitives, aperitives, abstersives, corrosives, restringents, palliatives, laxatives, cephalalgics, icterics, apophlegmatics, acoustics* (*Gulliver's Travels* by Jonathan Swift)

lest CONJ in case. If you do something lest something (usually) unpleasant happens you do it to try to prevent it happening ❑ *She went in without knocking, and hurried upstairs, in great fear lest she should meet the real Mary Ann* (*Alice's Adventures in Wonderland* by Lewis Carroll)

levee NOUN a levee is an old term for a meeting held in the morning, shortly after the person holding the meeting has got out of bed ❑ *I used to attend the King's levee once or twice a week* (*Gulliver's Travels* by Jonathan Swift)

life-preserver NOUN a club which had lead inside it to make it heavier and therefore more dangerous ❑ *and with no more suspicious articles displayed to view than two or three heavy bludgeons which stood in a corner, and a "life-preserver" that hung over the chimney-piece.* (*Oliver Twist* by Charles Dickens)

lighterman NOUN a lighterman is another word for sailor ❑ *in and out, hammers going in ship-builders' yards, saws going at timber, clashing engines going at things unknown, pumps going in leaky ships, capstans going, ships going out to sea, and unintelligible sea creatures roaring curses over the bulwarks at respondent lightermen* (*Great Expectations* by Charles Dickens)

livery NOUN servants often wore a uniform known as a livery ❑ *suddenly a footman in livery came running out of the wood* (*Alice's Adventures in Wonderland* by Lewis Carroll)

livid ADJ livid means pale or ash coloured. Livid also means very angry ❑ *a dirty, livid white* (*Treasure Island* by Robert Louis Stevenson)

lottery-tickets NOUN a popular card game ❑ *and Mrs. Philips protested that they would have a nice comfortable noisy game of lottery tickets* (*Pride and Prejudice* by Jane Austen)

lower and upper world PHRASE the earth and the heavens are the lower and upper worlds ❑ *the changes in the lower and upper world* (*Gulliver's Travels* by Jonathan Swift)

lustres NOUN lustres are chandeliers. A chandelier is a large, decorative frame which holds light bulbs or candles and hangs from the ceiling ❑ *the lustres, lights, the carving and the guilding* (*The Prelude* by William Wordsworth)

lynched VERB killed without a criminal trial by a crowd of people ❑ *He'll never know how nigh he come to getting lynched* (*The Adventures of Huckleberry Finn* by Mark Twain)

malingering VERB if someone is malingering they are pretending to be ill to avoid working ❑ *And you stand there malingering* (*Treasure Island* by Robert Louis Stevenson)

managing PHRASE treating with consideration ❑ *to think the honour of my own kind not worth managing* (*Gulliver's Travels* by Jonathan Swift)

manhood PHRASE manhood means human nature ❑ *concerning the nature of manhood* (*Gulliver's Travels* by Jonathan Swift)

man-trap NOUN a man-trap is a set of steel jaws that snap shut when trodden on and trap a person's leg

❑ *"Don't go to him," I called out of the window, "he's an assassin! A man-trap!"* (Oliver Twist by Charles Dickens)

maps NOUN charts of the night sky ❑ *Let maps to others, worlds on worlds have shown* (The Good-Morrow by John Donne)

mark VERB look at or notice ❑ *Mark but this flea, and mark in this* (The Flea by John Donne)

maroons NOUN A maroon is someone who has been left in a place which it is difficult for them to escape from, like a small island ❑ *if schooners, islands, and maroons* (Treasure Island by Robert Louis Stevenson)

mast NOUN here mast means the fruit of forest trees ❑ *a quantity of acorns, dates, chestnuts, and other mast* (Gulliver's Travels by Jonathan Swift)

mate VERB defeat ❑ *Where Mars did mate the warlike Carthigens* (Doctor Faustus Chorus by Christopher Marlowe)

mealy ADJ Mealy when used to describe a face meant pallid, pale or colourless ❑ *I only know two sorts of boys. Mealy boys, and beef-faced boys* (Oliver Twist by Charles Dickens)

middling ADV fairly or moderately ❑ *she worked me middling hard for about an hour* (The Adventures of Huckleberry Finn by Mark Twain)

mill NOUN a mill, or treadmill, was a device for hard labour or punishment in prison ❑ *Was you never on the mill?* (Oliver Twist by Charles Dickens)

milliner's shop NOUN a milliner's sold fabrics, clothing, lace and accessories; as time went on they specialized more and more in hats ❑ *to pay their duty to their aunt and to a milliner's shop just over the way* (Pride and Prejudice by Jane Austen)

minching un' munching PHRASE how people in the north of England used to describe the Way people

from the south speak ❑ *Minching un' munching!* (Wuthering Heights by Emily Brontë)

mine NOUN gold ❑ *Whether both th'Indias of spice and mine* (The Sun Rising by John Donne)

mire NOUN mud ❑ *Tis my fate to be always ground into the mire under the iron heel of oppression* (The Adventures of Huckleberry Finn by Mark Twain)

miscellany NOUN a miscellany is a collection of many different kinds of things ❑ *under that, the miscellany began* (Treasure Island by Robert Louis Stevenson)

mistarshers NOUN mistarshers means moustache, which is the hair that grows on a man's upper lip ❑ *when he put his hand up to his mistarshers* (Tess of the D'Urbervilles by Thomas Hardy)

morrow NOUN here good-morrow means tomorrow and a new and better life ❑ *And now good-morrow to our waking souls* (The Good-Morrow by John Donne)

mortification NOUN mortification is an old word for gangrene which is when part of the body decays or "dies" because of disease ❑ *Yes, it was a mortification–that was it* (The Adventures of Huckleberry Finn by Mark Twain)

mought VERB mought is an old spelling of might ❑ *what you mought call me? You mought call me captain* (Treasure Island by Robert Louis Stevenson)

move VERB move me not means do not make me angry ❑ *Move me not, Faustus* (Doctor Faustus 2.1 by Christopher Marlowe)

muffin-cap NOUN a muffin-cap is a flat cap made from wool ❑ *the old one, remained stationary in the muffin-cap and leathers* (Oliver Twist by Charles Dickens)

mulatter NOUN a mulatter was another word for mulatto, which is a person with parents who are from different races ❑ *a mulatter, most as white as a white man* (*The Adventures of Huckleberry Finn* by Mark Twain)

mummery NOUN mummery is an old word that meant meaningless (or pretentious) ceremony ❑ *When they were all gone, and when Trabb and his men–but not his boy: I looked for him–had crammed their mummery into bags, and were gone too, the house felt wholesomer.* (*Great Expectations* by Charles Dickens)

nap NOUN the nap is the woolly surface on a new item of clothing. Here the surface has been worn away so it looks bare ❑ *like an old hat with the nap rubbed off* (*The Adventures of Huckleberry Finn* by Mark Twain)

natural ■ NOUN a natural is a person born with learning difficulties ❑ *though he had been left to his particular care by their deceased father, who thought him almost a natural.* (*David Copperfield* by Charles Dickens) ■ ADJ natural meant illegitimate ❑ *Harriet Smith was the natural daughter of somebody* (*Emma* by Jane Austen)

navigator NOUN a navigator was originally someone employed to dig canals. It is the origin of the word "navvy" meaning a labourer ❑ *She ascertained from me in a few words what it was all about, comforted Dora, and gradually convinced her that I was not a labourer–from my manner of stating the case I believe Dora concluded that I was a navigator, and went balancing myself up and down a plank all day with a wheelbarrow–and so brought us together in peace.* (*David Copperfield* by Charles Dickens)

necromancy NOUN necromancy means a kind of magic where the magician speaks to spirits or ghosts to find out what will happen in the future ❑ *He surfeits upon cursed necromancy* (*Doctor Faustus chorus* by Christopher Marlowe)

negus NOUN a negus is a hot drink made from sweetened wine and water ❑ *He sat placidly perusing the newspaper, with his little head on one side, and a glass of warm sherry negus at his elbow.* (*David Copperfield* by Charles Dickens)

nice ADJ discriminating. Able to make good judgements or choices ❑ *consequently a claim to be nice* (*Emma* by Jane Austen)

nigh ADV nigh means near ❑ *He'll never know how nigh he come to getting lynched* (*The Adventures of Huckleberry Finn* by Mark Twain)

nimbleness NOUN nimbleness means being able to move very quickly or skilfully ❑ *and with incredible accuracy and nimbleness* (*Treasure Island* by Robert Louis Stevenson)

noggin NOUN a noggin is a small mug or a wooden cup ❑ *you'll bring me one noggin of rum* (*Treasure Island* by Robert Louis Stevenson)

none ADJ neither ❑ *none can die* (*The Good-Morrow* by John Donne)

notices NOUN observations ❑ *Arch are his notices* (*The Prelude* by William Wordsworth)

occiput NOUN occiput means the back of the head ❑ *saw off the occiput of each couple* (*Gulliver's Travels* by Jonathan Swift)

officiously ADV kindly ❑ *the governess who attended Glumdalclitch very officiously lifted me up* (*Gulliver's Travels* by Jonathan Swift)

old salt PHRASE old salt is a slang term for an experienced sailor ❑ *a "true sea-dog", and a "real old salt"* (*Treasure Island* by Robert Louis Stevenson)

or ere PHRASE before ❑ *or ere the Hall was built* (*The Prelude* by William Wordsworth)

ostler NOUN one who looks after horses at an inn ❑ *The bill paid, and the waiter remembered, and the ostler not forgotten, and the chambermaid taken into consideration* (*Great Expectations* by Charles Dickens)

ostry NOUN an ostry is an old word for a pub or hotel ❏ *lest I send you into the ostry with a vengeance* (*Doctor Faustus 2.2* by Christopher Marlowe)

outrunning the constable PHRASE outrunning the constable meant spending more than you earn ❏ *but I shall by this means be able to check your bills and to pull you up if I find you outrunning the constable.* (*Great Expectations* by Charles Dickens)

over ADV across ❏ *It is in length six yards, and in the thickest part at least three yards over* (*Gulliver's Travels* by Jonathan Swift)

over the broomstick PHRASE this is a phrase meaning "getting married without a formal ceremony" ❏ *They both led tramping lives, and this woman in Gerrard-street here, had been married very young, over the broomstick (as we say), to a tramping man, and was a perfect fury in point of jealousy.* (*Great Expectations* by Charles Dickens)

own VERB own means to admit or to acknowledge ❏ *It's my old girl that advises. She has the head. But I never own to it before her. Discipline must be maintained* (*Bleak House* by Charles Dickens)

page NOUN here page means a boy employed to run errands ❏ *not my feigned page* (*On His Mistress* by John Donne)

paid pretty dear PHRASE paid pretty dear means paid a high price or suffered quite a lot ❏ *I paid pretty dear for my monthly fourpenny piece* (*Treasure Island* by Robert Louis Stevenson)

pannikins NOUN pannikins were small tin cups ❏ *of lifting light glasses and cups to his lips, as if they were clumsy pannikins* (*Great Expectations* by Charles Dickens)

pards NOUN pards are leopards ❏ *Not charioted by Bacchus and his pards* (*Ode on a Nightingale* by John Keats)

parlour boarder NOUN a pupil who lived with the family ❏ *and somebody had lately raised her from the condition of scholar to parlour boarder* (*Emma* by Jane Austen)

particular, a London PHRASE London in Victorian times and up to the 1950s was famous for having very dense fog–which was a combination of real fog and the smog of pollution from factories ❏ *This is a London particular . . . A fog, miss* (*Bleak House* by Charles Dickens)

patten NOUN pattens were wooden soles which were fixed to shoes by straps to protect the shoes in wet weather ❏ *carrying a basket like the Great Seal of England in plaited straw, a pair of pattens, a spare shawl, and an umbrella, though it was a fine bright day* (*Great Expectations* by Charles Dickens)

paviour NOUN a paviour was a labourer who worked on the street pavement ❏ *the paviour his pickaxe* (*Oliver Twist* by Charles Dickens)

peccant ADJ peccant means unhealthy ❏ *other peccant humours* (*Gulliver's Travels* by Jonathan Swift)

penetralium NOUN penetralium is a word used to describe the inner rooms of the house ❏ *and I had no desire to aggravate his impatience previous to inspecting the penetralium* (*Wuthering Heights* by Emily Brontë)

pensive ADV pensive means deep in thought or thinking seriously about something ❏ *and she was leaning pensive on a tomb-stone on her right elbow* (*The Adventures of Huckleberry Finn* by Mark Twain)

penury NOUN penury is the state of being extremely poor ❏ *Distress, if not penury, loomed in the distance* (*Tess of the D'Urbervilles* by Thomas Hardy)

perspective NOUN telescope ❏ *a pocket perspective* (*Gulliver's Travels* by Jonathan Swift)

phaeton NOUN a phaeton was an open carriage for four people ❏ *often* *condescends to drive by my humble abode in her little phaeton and ponies* (*Pride and Prejudice* by Jane Austen)

phantasm NOUN a phantasm is an illusion, something that is not real. It is sometimes used to mean ghost ❏ *Experience had bred no fancies in him that could raise the phantasm of appetite* (*Silas Marner* by George Eliot)

physic NOUN here physic means medicine ❏ *there I studied physic two years and seven months* (*Gulliver's Travels* by Jonathan Swift)

pinioned VERB to pinion is to hold both arms so that a person cannot move them ❏ *But the relentless Ghost pinioned him in both his arms, and forced him to observe what happened next.* (*A Christmas Carol* by Charles Dickens)

piquet NOUN piquet was a popular card game in the C18th ❏ *Mr Hurst and Mr Bingley were at piquet* (*Pride and Prejudice* by Jane Austen)

plaister NOUN a plaister is a piece of cloth on which an apothecary (or pharmacist) would spread ointment. The cloth is then applied to wounds or bruises to treat them ❏ *Then, she gave the knife a final smart wipe on the edge of the plaister, and then sawed a very thick round off the loaf: which she finally, before separating from the loaf, hewed into two halves, of which Joe got one, and I the other.* (*Great Expectations* by Charles Dickens)

plantations NOUN here plantations means colonies, which are countries controlled by a more powerful country ❏ *besides our plantations in America* (*Gulliver's Travels* by Jonathan Swift)

plastic ADJ here plastic is an old term meaning shaping or a power that was forming ❏ *A plastic power abode with me* (*The Prelude* by William Wordsworth)

players NOUN actors ❏ *of players which upon the world's stage be* (*On His Mistress* by John Donne)

plump ADV all at once, suddenly ❏ *But it took a bit of time to get it well round, the change come so uncommon plump, didn't it?* (*Great Expectations* by Charles Dickens)

plundered VERB to plunder is to rob or steal from ❏ *These crosses stand for the names of ships or towns that they sank or plundered* (*Treasure Island* by Robert Louis Stevenson)

pommel ■ VERB to pommel someone is to hit them repeatedly with your fists ❏ *hug him round the neck, pommel his back, and kick his legs in irrepressible affection!* (*A Christmas Carol* by Charles Dickens) ■ NOUN a pommel is the part of a saddle that rises up at the front ❏ *He had his gun across his pommel* (*The Adventures of Huckleberry Finn* by Mark Twain)

poor's rates NOUN poor's rates were property taxes which were used to support the poor ❏ *"Oh!" replied the undertaker; "why, you know, Mr. Bumble, I pay a good deal towards the poor's rates."* (*Oliver Twist* by Charles Dickens)

popular ADJ popular means ruled by the people, or Republican, rather than ruled by a monarch ❏ *With those of Greece compared and popular Rome* (*The Prelude* by William Wordsworth)

porringer NOUN a porringer is a small bowl ❏ *Of this festive composition each boy had one porringer, and no more* (*Oliver Twist* by Charles Dickens)

postboy NOUN a postboy was the driver of a horse-drawn carriage ❏ *He spoke to a postboy who was dozing under the gateway* (*Oliver Twist* by Charles Dickens)

post-chaise NOUN a fast carriage for two or four passengers ❏ *Looking round, he saw that it was a post-chaise, driven at great speed* (*Oliver Twist* by Charles Dickens)

postern NOUN a small gate usually at the back of a building ❏ *The little servant happening to be entering the* fortress with two hot rolls, I passed through the postern and crossed the drawbridge, in her company (*Great Expectations* by Charles Dickens)

pottle NOUN a pottle was a small basket ❏ *He had a paper-bag under each arm and a pottle of strawberries in one hand . . .* (*Great Expectations* by Charles Dickens)

pounce NOUN pounce is a fine powder used to prevent ink spreading on untreated paper ❏ *in that grim atmosphere of pounce and parchment, red-tape, dusty wafers, ink-jars, brief and draft paper, law reports, writs, declarations, and bills of costs* (*David Copperfield* by Charles Dickens)

pox NOUN pox means sexually transmitted diseases like syphilis ❏ *how the pox in all its consequences and denominations* (*Gulliver's Travels* by Jonathan Swift)

prelibation NOUN prelibation means a foretaste of or an example of something to come ❏ *A prelibation to the mower's scythe* (*The Prelude* by William Wordsworth)

prentice NOUN an apprentice ❏ *and Joe, sitting on an old gun, had told me that when I was 'prentice to him regularly bound, we would have such Larks there!* (*Great Expectations* by Charles Dickens)

presently ADV immediately ❏ *I presently knew what they meant* (*Gulliver's Travels* by Jonathan Swift)

pumpion NOUN pumpkin ❏ *for it was almost as large as a small pumpion* (*Gulliver's Travels* by Jonathan Swift)

punctual ADJ kept in one place ❏ *was not a punctual presence, but a spirit* (*The Prelude* by William Wordsworth)

quadrille ■ NOUN a quadrille is a dance invented in France which is usually performed by four couples ❏ *However, Mr Swiveller had Miss Sophy's hand for the first quadrille* (country-dances being low, were utterly proscribed) (*The Old Curiosity Shop* by Charles Dickens) ■ NOUN quadrille was a card game for four people ❏ *to make up her pool of quadrille in the evening* (*Pride and Prejudice* by Jane Austen)

quality NOUN gentry or upper-class people ❏ *if you are with the quality* (*The Adventures of Huckleberry Finn* by Mark Twain)

quick parts PHRASE quick-witted ❏ *Mr Bennet was so odd a mixture of quick parts* (*Pride and Prejudice* by Jane Austen)

quid NOUN a quid is something chewed or kept in the mouth, like a piece of tobacco ❏ *rolling his quid* (*Treasure Island* by Robert Louis Stevenson)

quit VERB quit means to avenge or to make even ❏ *But Faustus's death shall quit my infamy* (*Doctor Faustus 4.3* by Christopher Marlowe)

rags NOUN divisions ❏ *Nor hours, days, months, which are the rags of time* (*The Sun Rising* by John Donne)

raiment NOUN raiment means clothing ❏ *the mountain shook off turf and flower, had only heath for raiment and crag for gem* (*Jane Eyre* by Charlotte Brontë)

rain cats and dogs PHRASE an expression meaning rain heavily. The origin of the expression is unclear ❏ *But it'll perhaps rain cats and dogs to-morrow* (*Silas Marner* by George Eliot)

raised Cain PHRASE raised Cain means caused a lot of trouble. Cain is a character in the Bible who killed his brother Abel ❏ *and every time he got drunk he raised Cain around town* (*The Adventures of Huckleberry Finn* by Mark Twain)

rambling ADJ rambling means confused and not very clear ❏ *my head began to be filled very early with rambling thoughts* (*Robinson Crusoe* by Daniel Defoe)

raree-show NOUN a raree-show is an old term for a peep-show or a fairground entertainment ❑ *A raree-show is here, with children gathered round* (*The Prelude* by William Wordsworth)

recusants NOUN people who resisted authority ❑ *hardy recusants* (*The Prelude* by William Wordsworth)

redounding VERB eddying. An eddy is a movement in water or air which goes round and round instead of flowing in one direction ❑ *mists and steam-like fogs redounding everywhere* (*The Prelude* by William Wordsworth)

redundant ADJ here redundant means overflowing but Wordsworth also uses it to mean excessively large or too big ❑ *A tempest, a redundant energy* (*The Prelude* by William Wordsworth)

reflex NOUN reflex is a shortened version of reflexion, which is an alternative spelling of reflection ❑ *To cut across the reflex of a star* (*The Prelude* by William Wordsworth)

Reformatory NOUN a prison for young offenders/criminals ❑ *Even when I was taken to have a new suit of clothes, the tailor had orders to make them like a kind of Reformatory, and on no account to let me have the free use of my limbs.* (*Great Expectations* by Charles Dickens)

remorse NOUN pity or compassion ❑ *by that remorse* (*On His Mistress* by John Donne)

render VERB in this context render means give. ❑ *and Sarah could render no reason that would be sanctioned by the feeling of the community.* (*Silas Marner* by George Eliot)

repeater NOUN a repeater was a watch that chimed the last hour when a button was pressed–as a result it was useful in the dark ❑ *And his watch is a gold repeater, and worth a hundred pound if it's worth a penny.* (*Great Expectations* by Charles Dickens)

repugnance NOUN repugnance means a strong dislike of something or someone ❑ *overcoming a strong repugnance* (*Treasure Island* by Robert Louis Stevenson)

reverence NOUN reverence means bow. When you bow to someone, you briefly bend your body towards them as a formal way of showing them respect ❑ *made my reverence* (*Gulliver's Travels* by Jonathan Swift)

reverie NOUN a reverie is a daydream ❑ *I can guess the subject of your reverie* (*Pride and Prejudice* by Jane Austen)

revival NOUN a religious meeting held in public ❑ *well I'd ben a-running' a little temperance revival thar' bout a week* (*The Adventures of Huckleberry Finn* by Mark Twain)

revolt VERB revolt means turn back or stop your present course of action and go back to what you were doing before ❑ *Revolt, or I'll in piecemeal tear thy flesh* (*Doctor Faustus 5.1* by Christopher Marlowe)

rheumatics/rheumatism NOUN rheumatics [rheumatism] is an illness that makes your joints or muscles stiff and painful ❑ *a new cure for the rheumatics* (*Treasure Island* by Robert Louis Stevenson)

riddance NOUN riddance is usually used in the form good riddance which you say when you are pleased that something has gone or been left behind ❑ *I'd better go into the house, and die and be a riddance* (*David Copperfield* by Charles Dickens)

rimy ADJ rimy is an adjective which means covered in ice or frost ❑ *It was a rimy morning, and very damp* (*Great Expectations* by Charles Dickens)

riper ADJ riper means more mature or older ❑ *At riper years to Wittenberg he went* (*Doctor Faustus chorus* by Christopher Marlowe)

rubber NOUN a set of games in whist or backgammon ❑ *her father was sure of his rubber* (*Emma* by Jane Austen)

ruffian NOUN a ruffian is a person who behaves violently ❑ *and when the ruffian had told him* (*Treasure Island* by Robert Louis Stevenson)

sadness NOUN sadness is an old term meaning seriousness ❑ *But I prithee tell me, in good sadness* (*Doctor Faustus 2.2* by Christopher Marlowe)

sailed before the mast PHRASE this phrase meant someone who did not look like a sailor ❑ *he had none of the appearance of a man that sailed before the mast* (*Treasure Island* by Robert Louis Stevenson)

scabbard NOUN a scabbard is the covering for a sword or dagger ❑ *Girded round its middle was an antique scabbard; but no sword was in it, and the ancient sheath was eaten up with rust* (*A Christmas Carol* by Charles Dickens)

schooners NOUN A schooner is a fast, medium-sized sailing ship ❑ *if schooners, islands, and maroons* (*Treasure Island* by Robert Louis Stevenson)

science NOUN learning or knowledge ❑ *Even Science, too, at hand* (*The Prelude* by William Wordsworth)

scrouge VERB to scrouge means to squeeze or to crowd ❑ *to scrouge in and get a sight* (*The Adventures of Huckleberry Finn* by Mark Twain)

scrutore NOUN a scrutore, or escritoire, was a writing table ❑ *set me gently on my feet upon the scrutore* (*Gulliver's Travels* by Jonathan Swift)

scutcheon/escutcheon NOUN an escutcheon is a shield with a coat of arms, or the symbols of a family name, engraved on it ❑ *On the scutcheon we'll have a bend* (*The Adventures of Huckleberry Finn* by Mark Twain)

sea-dog PHRASE sea-dog is a slang term for an experienced sailor or pirate

❑ *a "true sea-dog", and a "real old salt,"* (*Treasure Island* by Robert Louis Stevenson)

see the lions PHRASE to see the lions was to go and see the sights of London. Originally the phrase referred to the menagerie in the Tower of London and later in Regent's Park ❑ *We will go and see the lions for an hour or two–it's something to have a fresh fellow like you to show them to, Copperfield* (*David Copperfield* by Charles Dickens)

self-conceit NOUN self-conceit is an old term which means having too high an opinion of oneself, or deceiving yourself ❑ *Till swollen with cunning, of a self-conceit* (*Doctor Faustus chorus* by Christopher Marlowe)

seneschal NOUN a steward ❑ *where a grey-headed seneschal sings a funny chorus with a funnier body of vassals* (*Oliver Twist* by Charles Dickens)

sensible ADJ if you were sensible of something you are aware or conscious of something ❑ *If my children are silly I must hope to be always sensible of it* (*Pride and Prejudice* by Jane Austen)

sessions NOUN court cases were heard at specific times of the year called sessions ❑ *He lay in prison very ill, during the whole interval between his committal for trial, and the coming round of the Sessions.* (*Great Expectations* by Charles Dickens)

shabby ADJ shabby places look old and in bad condition ❑ *a little bit of a shabby village named Pikesville* (*The Adventures of Huckleberry Finn* by Mark Twain)

shay-cart NOUN a shay-cart was a small cart drawn by one horse ❑ *"I were at the Bargemen t'other night, Pip;" whenever he subsided into affection, he called me Pip, and whenever he relapsed into politeness he called me Sir; "when there come up in his* *shay-cart Pumblechook." (Great Expectations* by Charles Dickens)

shilling NOUN a shilling is an old unit of currency. There were twenty shillings in every British pound ❑ *"Ten shillings too much," said the gentleman in the white waistcoat. (Oliver Twist* by Charles Dickens)

shines NOUN tricks or games ❑ *well, it would make a cow laugh to see the shines that old idiot cut (The Adventures of Huckleberry Finn* by Mark Twain)

shirking VERB shirking means not doing what you are meant to be doing, or evading your duties ❑ *some of you shirking lubbers (Treasure Island* by Robert Louis Stevenson)

shiver my timbers PHRASE shiver my timbers is an expression which was used by sailors and pirates to express surprise ❑ *why, shiver my timbers, if I hadn't forgotten my score! (Treasure Island* by Robert Louis Stevenson)

shoe-roses NOUN shoe-roses were roses made from ribbons which were stuck on to shoes as decoration ❑ *the very shoe-roses for Netherfield were got by proxy (Pride and Prejudice* by Jane Austen)

singular ADJ singular means very great and remarkable or strange ❑ *"Singular dream," he says (The Adventures of Huckleberry Finn* by Mark Twain)

sire NOUN sire is an old word which means lord or master or elder ❑ *She also defied her sire (Little Women* by Louisa May Alcott)

sixpence NOUN a sixpence was half of a shilling ❑ *if she had only a shilling in the world, she would be very lilkely to give away sixpence of it (Emma* by Jane Austen)

slavey NOUN the word slavey was used when there was only one servant in a house or boarding-house–so she had to perform all the duties of a larger staff ❑ *Two distinct knocks, sir, will produce the slavey at any*

time (The Old Curiosity Shop by Charles Dickens)

slender ADJ weak ❑ *In slender accents of sweet verse (The Prelude* by William Wordsworth)

slop-shops NOUN slop-shops were shops where cheap ready-made clothes were sold. They mainly sold clothes to sailors ❑ *Accordingly, I took the jacket off, that I might learn to do without it; and carrying it under my arm, began a tour of inspection of the various slop-shops. (David Copperfield* by Charles Dickens)

sluggard NOUN a lazy person ❑ *"Stand up and repeat 'Tis the voice of the sluggard,'" said the Gryphon. (Alice's Adventures in Wonderland* by Lewis Carroll)

smallpox NOUN smallpox is a serious infectious disease ❑ *by telling the men we had smallpox aboard (The Adventures of Huckleberry Finn* by Mark Twain)

smalls NOUN smalls are short trousers ❑ *It is difficult for a large-headed, small-eyed youth, of lumbering make and heavy countenance, to look dignified under any circumstances; but it is more especially so, when superadded to these personal attractions are a red nose and yellow smalls (Oliver Twist* by Charles Dickens)

sneeze-box NOUN a box for snuff was called a sneeze-box because sniffing snuff makes the user sneeze ❑ *To think of Jack Dawkins—lummy Jack —the Dodger—the Artful Dodger— going abroad for a common twopenny-halfpenny sneeze-box! (Oliver Twist* by Charles Dickens)

snorted VERB slept ❑ *Or snorted we in the Seven Sleepers' den? (The Good-Morrow* by John Donne)

snuff NOUN snuff is tobacco in powder form which is taken by sniffing ❑ *as he thrust his thumb and fore-finger into the proffered snuff-box of the undertaker: which was an ingenious little model of a patent* *coffin.* (*Oliver Twist* by Charles Dickens)

soliloquized VERB to soliloquize is when an actor in a play speaks to himself or herself rather than to another actor ❏ *"A new servitude! There is something in that," I soliloquized (mentally, be it understood; I did not talk aloud)* (*Jane Eyre* by Charlotte Brontë)

sough NOUN a sough is a drain or a ditch ❏ *as you may have noticed the sough that runs from the marshes* (*Wuthering Heights* by Emily Brontë)

spirits NOUN a spirit is the nonphysical part of a person which is believed to remain alive after their death ❏ *that I might raise up spirits when I please* (*Doctor Faustus* 1.5 by Christopher Marlowe)

spleen ■ NOUN here spleen means a type of sadness or depression which was thought to only affect the wealthy ❏ *yet here I could plainly discover the true seeds of spleen* (*Gulliver's Travels* by Jonathan Swift) ■ NOUN irritability and low spirits ❏ *Adieu to disappointment and spleen* (*Pride and Prejudice* by Jane Austen)

spondulicks NOUN spondulicks is a slang word which means money ❏ *not for all his spondulicks and as much more on top of it* (*The Adventures of Huckleberry Finn* by Mark Twain)

stalled of VERB to be stalled of something is to be bored with it ❏ *I'm stalled of doing naught* (*Wuthering Heights* by Emily Brontë)

stanchion NOUN a stanchion is a pole or bar that stands upright and is used as a building support ❏ *and slid down a stanchion* (*The Adventures of Huckleberry Finn* by Mark Twain)

stang NOUN stang is another word for pole which was an old measurement ❏ *These fields were intermingled with woods of half a stang* (*Gulliver's Travels* by Jonathan Swift)

starlings NOUN a starling is a wall built around the pillars that support a bridge to protect the pillars ❏ *There were states of the tide when, having been down the river, I could not get back through the eddy-chafed arches and starlings of old London Bridge* (*Great Expectations* by Charles Dickens)

startings NOUN twitching or night-time movements of the body ❏ *with midnight's startings* (*On His Mistress* by John Donne)

stomacher NOUN a panel at the front of a dress ❏ *but send her aunt the pattern of a stomacher* (*Emma* by Jane Austen)

stoop VERB swoop ❏ *Once a kite hovering over the garden made a stoop at me* (*Gulliver's Travels* by Jonathan Swift)

succedaneum NOUN a succedaneum is a substitute ❏ *But as a succedaneum* (*The Prelude* by William Wordsworth)

suet NOUN a hard animal fat used in cooking ❏ *and your jaws are too weak For anything tougher than suet* (*Alice's Adventures in Wonderland* by Lewis Carroll)

sultry ADJ sultry weather is hot and damp. Here sultry means unpleasant or risky ❏ *for it was getting pretty sultry for us* (*The Adventures of Huckleberry Finn* by Mark Twain)

summerset NOUN summerset is an old spelling of somersault. If someone does a somersault, they turn over completely in the air ❏ *I have seen him do the summerset* (*Gulliver's Travels* by Jonathan Swift)

supper NOUN supper was a light meal taken late in the evening. The main meal was dinner which was eaten at four or five in the afternoon ❏ *and the supper table was all set out* (*Emma* by Jane Austen)

surfeits VERB to surfeit in something is to have far too much of it, or to overindulge in it to an unhealthy degree ❏ *He surfeits upon cursed* necromancy (*Doctor Faustus chorus* by Christopher Marlowe)

surtout NOUN a surtout is a long close-fitting overcoat ❏ *He wore a long black surtout reaching nearly to his ankles* (*The Old Curiosity Shop* by Charles Dickens)

swath NOUN swath is the width of corn cut by a scythe ❏ *while thy hook Spares the next swath* (*Ode to Autumn* by John Keats)

sylvan ADJ sylvan means belonging to the woods ❏ *Sylvan historian* (*Ode on a Grecian Urn* by John Keats)

taction NOUN taction means touch. This means that the people had to be touched on the mouth or the ears to get their attention ❏ *without being roused by some external taction upon the organs of speech and hearing* (*Gulliver's Travels* by Jonathan Swift)

Tag and Rag and Bobtail PHRASE the riff-raff, or lower classes. Used in an insulting way ❏ *"No," said he; "not till it got about that there was no protection on the premises, and it come to be considered dangerous, with convicts and Tag and Rag and Bobtail going up and down."* (*Great Expectations* by Charles Dickens)

tallow NOUN tallow is hard animal fat that is used to make candles and soap ❏ *and a lot of tallow candles* (*The Adventures of Huckleberry Finn* by Mark Twain)

tan VERB to tan means to beat or whip ❏ *and if I catch you about that school I'll tan you good* (*The Adventures of Huckleberry Finn* by Mark Twain)

tanyard NOUN the tanyard is part of a tannery, which is a place where leather is made from animal skins ❏ *hid in the old tanyard* (*The Adventures of Huckleberry Finn* by Mark Twain)

tarry ADJ tarry means the colour of tar or black ❏ *his tarry pig-tail*

(*Treasure Island* by Robert Louis Stevenson)

thereof PHRASE from there ❏ *By all desires which thereof did ensue* (*On His Mistress* by John Donne)

thick with, be PHRASE if you are "thick with someone" you are very close, sharing secrets–it is often used to describe people who are planning something secret ❏ *Hasn't he been thick with Mr Heathcliff lately?* (*Wuthering Heights* by Emily Brontë)

thimble NOUN a thimble is a small cover used to protect the finger while sewing ❏ *The paper had been sealed in several places by a thimble* (*Treasure Island* by Robert Louis Stevenson)

thirtover ADJ thirtover is an old word which means obstinate or that someone is very determined to do want they want and can not be persuaded to do something in another way ❏ *I have been living on in a thirtover, lackadaisical way* (*Tess of the D'Urbervilles* by Thomas Hardy)

timbrel NOUN timbrel is a tambourine ❏ *What pipes and timbrels?* (*Ode on a Grecian Urn* by John Keats)

tin NOUN tin is slang for money/cash ❏ *Then the plain question is, an't it a pity that this state of things should continue, and how much better would it be for the old gentleman to hand over a reasonable amount of tin, and make it all right and comfortable* (*The Old Curiosity Shop* by Charles Dickens)

tincture NOUN a tincture is a medicine made with alcohol and a small amount of a drug ❏ *with ink composed of a cephalic tincture* (*Gulliver's Travels* by Jonathan Swift)

tithe NOUN a tithe is a tax paid to the church ❏ *and held farms which, speaking from a spiritual point of view, paid highly-desirable tithes* (*Silas Marner* by George Eliot)

towardly ADJ a towardly child is dutiful or obedient ❑ *and a towardly child* (*Gulliver's Travels* by Jonathan Swift)

toys NOUN trifles are things which are considered to have little importance, value, or significance ❑ *purchase my life from them bysome bracelets, glass rings, and other toys* (*Gulliver's Travels* by Jonathan Swift)

tract NOUN a tract is a religious pamphlet or leaflet ❑ *and Joe Harper has a hymn-book and a tract* (*The Adventures of Huckleberry Finn* by Mark Twain)

train-oil NOUN train-oil is oil from whale blubber ❑ *The train-oil and gunpowder were shoved out of sight in a minute* (*Wuthering Heights* by Emily Brontë)

tribulation NOUN tribulation means the suffering or difficulty you experience in a particular situation ❑ *Amy was learning this distinction through much tribulation* (*Little Women* by Louisa May Alcott)

trivet NOUN a trivet is a three-legged stand for resting a pot or kettle ❑ *a pocket-knife in his right; and a pewter pot on the trivet* (*Oliver Twist* by Charles Dickens)

trot line NOUN a trot line is a fishing line to which a row of smaller fishing lines are attached ❑ *when he got along I was hard at it taking up a trot line* (*The Adventures of Huckleberry Finn* by Mark Twain)

troth NOUN oath or pledge ❑ *I wonder, by my troth* (*The Good-Morrow* by John Donne)

truckle NOUN a truckle bedstead is a bed that is on wheels and can be slid under another bed to save space ❑ *It rose under my hand, and the door yielded. Looking in, I saw a lighted candle on a table, a bench, and a mattress on a truckle bedstead.* (*Great Expectations* by Charles Dickens)

trump NOUN a trump is a good, reliable person who can be trusted ❑ *This lad Hawkins is a trump, I perceive* (*Treasure Island* by Robert Louis Stevenson)

tucker NOUN a tucker is a frilly lace collar which is worn around the neck ❑ *Whereat Scrooge's niece's sister—the plump one with the lace tucker: not the one with the roses—blushed.* (*A Christmas Carol* by Charles Dickens)

tureen NOUN a large bowl with a lid from which soup or vegetables are served ❑ *Waiting in a hot tureen!* (*Alice's Adventures in Wonderland* by Lewis Carroll)

turnkey NOUN a prison officer; jailer ❑ *As we came out of the prison through the lodge, I found that the great importance of my guardian was appreciated by the turnkeys, no less than by those whom they held in charge.* (*Great Expectations* by Charles Dickens)

turnpike NOUN the upkeep of many roads of the time was paid for by tolls (fees) collected at posts along the road. There was a gate to prevent people travelling further along the road until the toll had been paid. ❑ *Traddles, whom I have taken up by appointment at the turnpike, presents a dazzling combination of cream colour and light blue; and both he and Mr. Dick have a general effect about them of being all gloves.* (*David Copperfield* by Charles Dickens)

twas PHRASE it was ❑ *twas but a dream of thee* (*The Good-Morrow* by John Donne)

tyrannized VERB tyrannized means bullied or forced to do things against their will ❑ *for people would soon cease coming there to be tyrannized over and put down* (*Treasure Island* by Robert Louis Stevenson)

'un NOUN 'un is a slang term for one—usually used to refer to a person ❑ *She's been thinking the old 'un* (*David Copperfield* by Charles Dickens)

undistinguished ADJ undiscriminating or incapable of making a distinction between good and bad things ❑

their undistinguished appetite to devour everything (*Gulliver's Travels* by Jonathan Swift)

use NOUN habit ❑ *Though use make you apt to kill me* (*The Flea* by John Donne)

vacant ADJ vacant usually means empty, but here Wordsworth uses it to mean carefree ❑ *To vacant musing, unreproved neglect* (*The Prelude* by William Wordsworth)

valetudinarian NOUN one too concerned with his or her own health. ❑ *for having been a valetudinarian all his life* (*Emma* by Jane Austen)

vamp VERB vamp means to walk or tramp to somewhere ❑ *Well, vamp on to Marlott, will 'ee* (*Tess of the D'Urbervilles* by Thomas Hardy)

vapours NOUN the vapours is an old term which means unpleasant and strange thoughts, which make the person feel nervous and unhappy ❑ *and my head was full of vapours* (*Robinson Crusoe* by Daniel Defoe)

vegetables NOUN here vegetables means plants ❑ *the other vegetables are in the same proportion* (*Gulliver's Travels* by Jonathan Swift)

venturesome ADJ if you are venture-some you are willing to take risks ❑ *he must be either hopelessly stupid or a venturesome fool* (*Wuthering Heights* by Emily Brontë)

verily ADV verily means really or truly ❑ *though I believe verily* (*Robinson Crusoe* by Daniel Defoe)

vicinage NOUN vicinage is an area or the residents of an area ❑ *and to his thought the whole vicinage was haunted by her.* (*Silas Marner* by George Eliot)

victuals NOUN victuals means food ❑ *grumble a little over the victuals* (*The Adventures of Huckleberry Finn* by Mark Twain)

vintage NOUN vintage in this context means wine ❑ *Oh, for a draught of*

vintage! (*Ode on a Nightingale* by John Keats)

virtual ADJ here virtual means powerful or strong ❑ *had virtual faith* (*The Prelude* by William Wordsworth)

vittles NOUN vittles is a slang word which means food ❑ *There never was such a woman for givin' away vittles and drink* (*Little Women* by Louisa May Alcott)

voided straight PHRASE voided straight is an old expression which means emptied immediately ❑ *see the rooms be voided straight* (*Doctor Faustus 4.1* by Christopher Marlowe)

wainscot NOUN wainscot is wood panel lining in a room so wainscoted means a room lined with wooden panels ❑ *in the dark wainscoted parlor* (*Silas Marner* by George Eliot)

walking the plank PHRASE walking the plank was a punishment in which a prisoner would be made to walk along a plank on the side of the ship and fall into the sea, where they would be abandoned ❑ *about hanging, and walking the plank* (*Treasure Island* by Robert Louis Stevenson)

want VERB want means to be lacking or short of ❑ *The next thing wanted was to get the picture framed* (*Emma* by Jane Austen)

wanting ADJ wanting means lacking or missing ❑ *wanting two fingers of the left hand* (*Treasure Island* by Robert Louis Stevenson)

wanting, I was not PHRASE I was not wanting means I did not fail ❑ *I was not wanting to lay a founda-tion of religious knowledge in his mind* (*Robinson Crusoe* by Daniel Defoe)

ward NOUN a ward is, usually, a child who has been put under the protection of the court or a guardian for his or her protection ❑ *I call the Wards in Jarndcye. They* *are caged up with all the others.* (*Bleak House* by Charles Dickens)

waylay VERB to waylay someone is to lie in wait for them or to intercept them ❑ *I must go up the road and waylay him* (*The Adventures of Huckleberry Finn* by Mark Twain)

weazen NOUN weazen is a slang word for throat. It actually means shrivelled ❑ *You with a uncle too! Why, I knowed you at Gargery's when you was so small a wolf that I could have took your weazen betwixt this finger and thumb and chucked you away dead* (*Great Expectations* by Charles Dickens)

wery ■ ADV very ❑ *Be wery careful o' vidders all your life* (*Pickwick Papers* by Charles Dickens) ■ *See* wibrated

wherry NOUN wherry is a small swift rowing boat for one person ❑ *It was flood tide when Daniel Quilp sat himself down in the wherry to cross to the opposite shore.* (*The Old Curiosity Shop* by Charles Dickens)

whether PREP whether means which of the two in this example ❑ *we came in full view of a great island or continent (for we knew not whether)* (*Gulliver's Travels* by Jonathan Swift)

whetstone NOUN a whetstone is a stone used to sharpen knives and other tools ❑ *I dropped pap's whetstone there too* (*The Adventures of Huckleberry Finn* by Mark Twain)

wibrated VERB in Dickens's use of the English language "w" often replaces "v" when he is reporting speech. So here "wibrated" means "vibrated". In *Pickwick Papers* a judge asks Sam Weller (who constantly confuses the two letters) "Do you spell it with a 'v' or a 'w'?" to which Weller replies "That depends upon the taste and fancy of the speller, my Lord" ❑ *There are strings . . . in the human heart that had better not be wibrated* (*Barnaby Rudge* by Charles Dickens)

wicket NOUN a wicket is a little door in a larger entrance ❑ *Having rested*

here, for a minute or so, to collect a good burst of sobs and an imposing show of tears and terror, he knocked loudly at the wicket (*Oliver Twist* by Charles Dickens)

without CONJ without means unless ❑ *You don't know about me, without you have read a book by the name of The Adventures of Tom Sawyer* (*The Adventures of Huckleberry Finn* by Mark Twain)

wittles ■ NOUN wittles is a slang word which means food ❑ *I live on broken wittles–and I sleep on the coals* (*David Copperfield* by Charles Dickens) ■ *See* wibrated

woo VERB courts or forms a proper relationship with ❑ *before it woo* (*The Flea* by John Donne)

words, to have PHRASE if you have words with someone you have a disagreement or an argument ❑ *I do not want to have words with a young thing like you.* (*Black Beauty* by Anna Sewell)

workhouse NOUN workhouses were places where the homeless were given food and a place to live in return for doing very hard work ❑ *And the Union workhouses? demanded Scrooge. Are they still in operation?* (*A Christmas Carol* by Charles Dickens)

yawl NOUN a yawl is a small boat kept on a bigger boat for short trips. Yawl is also the name for a small fishing boat ❑ *She sent out her yawl, and we went aboard* (*The Adventures of Huckleberry Finn* by Mark Twain)

yeomanry NOUN the yeomanry was a collective term for the middle classes involved in agriculture ❑ *The yeomanry are precisely the order of people with whom I feel I can have nothing to do* (*Emma* by Jane Austen)

yonder ADV yonder means over there ❑ *all in the same second we seem to hear low voices in yonder!* (*The Adventures of Huckleberry Finn* by Mark Twain)